PROSES

PROSES

Incomparable Parables! Fabulous Fables! Cruel Tales!

GARRETT CAPLES

ILLUSTRATIONS BY COLTER JACOBSEN

WAVE BOOKS   SEATTLE/NEW YORK

Published by Wave Books

www.wavepoetry.com

Copyright © 2024 by Garrett Caples

Wave Books titles are distributed to the trade by
Consortium Book Sales and Distribution
Phone: 800-283-3572 / SAN 631-760x

Library of Congress Cataloging-in-Publication Data
Names: Caples, Garrett T., author.
Title: Proses : incomparable parables!
fabulous fables! cruel tales! / Garrett Caples.
Description: First edition. | Seattle : Wave Books, 2024.
Identifiers: LCCN 2023041553 | ISBN 9781950268979 (paperback)
Subjects: LCGFT: Short stories.
Classification: LCC PS3603.A662 P76 2024 | DDC 813/.6—dc23/eng/20230928
LC record available at https://lccn.loc.gov/2023041553

Designed by Crisis
Printed in the United States of America

9 8 7 6 5 4 3 2 1
First Edition

This book is for Andrew Joron and Brian Lucas.

THE THEREMINIST

3

STEP FOOT

19

HECTOR NICE

33

NONE NUNS

63

THE SNEEZE

71

THE LEMON

93

VYVYAN SOURMAN

107

A.V.O.M.W.E.P.

131

PAC-MAN FEVER

151

Acknowledgments

107

3.VII.39

"One is Also a Powet"

"Unfortunately I have to add that one is also what the literati term a powet. This is so bloody embarrassing and inconvenient," as [George] Barker says in one of his letters.

One is impelled by a kind of pretentiousness so incredible that it simply has to be taken seriously.

One is "a powet." But this may not mean that one's existence is wholly centered round the mere writing of poems. I would rather say: I am dominated by a vociferous imagination, a turbulent creature which inhabits me; whose continual demand, allowing me no rest, is to be fed. The writing of poetry corresponds only to the digestive process of this monster. My life is dedicated to its nourishment.

David Gascoyne, *Collected Journals 1936–42*

THE THEREMINIST

". . . a marginally smaller and greener Tater."

I am seven years older than Andrew Joron was when we first met some 25 years ago. In that time, I have grown old, fat, ridiculous, while Andrew—I won't say looks *the same*—he certainly looks older—but he looks *just as well* as he did at age 40. Imperially slim, full head of hair, the same Germanic frown of inquiry constituting his face at rest, set off at the chin by a dashing cluster of thin white scars owing to a horrific boating accident as a child in Stuttgart. This habitual expression shows to best advantage during Andrew's performances on theremin, making him look stoic almost as he gesticulates like a crazed Wagnerian 10 hours into the Ring.

The theremin was a gift for his 50th birthday; a bunch of his friends, myself included, chipped in for the instrument that Andrew had long admired both for its surrealistic properties—it's the instrument you play but don't touch—and for its evocation of the science fiction of his youth. Still, as a nonmusician, he was, I fancied, almost intimidated by it, though he began dutifully investigating its sonic properties and occasionally reporting his findings in poetic settings.

But what changed everything was the return to the Bay Area of our friend Brian Lucas, after a six-year stint in Bangkok cave diving. Brian is a triple threat—poet, painter, musician—and being an old hand at being in bands, he soon had Andy jamming, then playing in a trio called Free Rein, which became a quartet called Cloud Shepherd. In the process, Andrew definitely became a musician, however free or outside. Cloud Shepherd is no more, but like every improv musician, Andrew's now in a hundred different bands of varying degrees of notoriety. Ostrich Nostril, Man the Fingerguns, Crow Crash Radio, they proliferate like Tribbles; he's even in one with Clark Coolidge on drums called Ouroboros.

And much like Tribbles, these bands are trouble. Always a deliberate writer, fastidious in output, Andrew has had to relax his literary productivity even further to accommodate these bands, an invasive species in a creative field hitherto devoted to writing. If this is a midlife crisis, it's an extraordinarily avant-garde one. New Andrew Joron poems appear at ever greater intervals; his publisher curses his apparent indolence, and I sometimes wonder if his friends and I are to blame for having bought him the theremin, or more likely whether it's Brian's fault for teaching him to jam. Have we inadvertently altered the course of literary history by reducing the eventual sum of Andrew Joron books? I myself am perfectly willing to accept a certain portion of his output in theremin, but will literary posterity ever forgive *me*?

Well, I've got my own problems, so it was only a matter of time before my concern for Andrew's decreased rate of literary production became a meditation on the related matter of how to turn the situation to my advantage. To wit: some time ago, during one of those speculative conversations two poets might have touching on future projects, Andrew mentioned he wanted to publish a book of prose called *Proses*. I thought this was splendid, and cheered on the idea, but the fact is he hasn't published such a volume in the intervening years, and perhaps indeed had mentioned it as a passing fancy, a funny idea rather than a serious endeavor.

It's funny because it underlines the fact that *prose* is a mass noun, though frequently placed in opposition to the count noun *poem*. In truth, one might say, *prose* is in opposition to *poetry*, but then there's no equivalent for an individual unit of prose as there is for an individual unit of poetry. But this essentially grammatical joke nonetheless takes on the air of an empirical one, as if the difference in the way the terms worked somehow reflected the distinction between poetry and prose.

Meanwhile, I myself was contemplating putting together a volume of prose of uncertain genre; the pieces were stories, yes, but I found myself resisting the label of "short story," associating it as I did with the moribund contemporary magazine fiction that dominated the popular conception of that term. To me, the pieces seemed more allied with poetry than with fiction, but they weren't really "prose poems" either, and so I cycled through various terms like "fables," "parables," or even "fairy tales," though none of these designations seemed to quite encompass the assemblage of poet's prose I had in mind. But *Proses*, I thought, would be an ideal title for such a book, highlighting the poet's versatility in the matter of writing prose.

Being a poet, I am, of course, an inveterate thief, and the prize was already in my possession; I merely needed to tell my own publisher, and the book would be announced and maybe even printed before Andrew would get wind of it. But even a cold-hearted fucker like me would hesitate to jack a title from my best friend without permission. Indeed, I'd already done this to him once inadvertently and felt badly about it; doing it again deliberately was a bridge too far.

I could, however, simply ask whether he still intended to use it and, if not, whether I could. So it was I found myself driving to his house in El Cerrito on a rare Saturday he wasn't tied up with one of his innumerable bands. His wife Rose answered the door and told me he was out back in his mancave. As I made my way through the kitchen to the backyard, I recalled that Rose's name was actually housed within the title *Proses* and I wondered whether this would make it even more difficult to dislodge from its owner. It's a characteristically Joron flourish, when he still condescends to write poems; the coincidence of diverse concepts bound together under the same or similar linguistic signs—accidents of chance and twenty-six letters—is one he exploits with at times astonishing dexterity, making us see not the standard collection of puns we rely on, but rather the "sun" rising out of "solace," the "agent" lurking in "angel." This rigorous unearthing of the possible connections lying fallow between and within words makes Andrew one of the great innovators of recent American poetry.

The mancave was a large toolshed Andrew had converted into his writing office, furnished with his computer, his LPs and CDs, and a significant portion of his library. More lately it had become his rehearsal space, the ever-present theremin and amplifier tucked into a corner when not in use. I could hear its high pitched quavering as I approached, even though he was alone. I knocked and the eerie sound abruptly ceased, replaced by rapid barking from his dog, a Chihuahua/Dachshund mix named Tater. Andrew opened the door and greeted me warmly, escorting me inside and offering me a Guinness from a still-cold six-pack awaiting my arrival. Tater trembled with his usual combination of excitement and nervousness. We caught up on various small matters, while Andrew from time to time dipped into a small tin of biscuits and tossed one to Tater, who gnawed on it while eyeing me warily.

Presently I got to the point: I had a prose book to do and I wanted to use his title, at least if he thought he wasn't going to use it himself. I explained how it fit the book I envisioned to a T, and how it was simply too funny a title to go unused. As I spoke, I searched his face for any sign as to how my request was landing, but I was unable to glean anything behind his Germanic frown of inquiry. At length, I exhausted my storehouse of phrases extolling our longstanding literary relationship, my regard for his poetic genius, the greatness of the title and its fitness for the purpose for which I wanted to use it, and gradually rolled to a halt, with little sense of what his thoughts might be.

After some moments of silent frowning, during which he scratched the small cluster of scars on his chin thoughtfully, unhurried by my raised eyebrow, he said yes, I could use the title.

"I need a favor, though," he said.

"Anything!" I said, ready to collapse with gratitude. Good ol' Andy!

"I need you to sign a contract," he said. He hesitated slightly before continuing. "It's for a project I'm working on."

"Right on," I said.

He turned to the computer and began to make a document. I helped myself to another Guinness while Tater continued to gnaw on his biscuit and eye me warily.

Presently I heard the dry murmur of paper rolling through the printer. Andrew plucked the page out of the tray and handed it to me. It read:

On this 7th day of October, in the earth year 20**, the undersigned purchaser, Garrett Caples, agrees to purchase the title *PROSES* from its coiner, Andrew Joron, in exchange for the sum of US$1.00.

Garrett Caples, Poet

Andrew Joron, Thereminist

It seemed harmless enough. He was clearly on some Bruce Conner, Duchamp type of shit, creating an assemblage of art and documentation. And "earth year" was just like him; he'd been writing science fiction of late, restricting his conventional poetic output further still. I approved of this writing so I didn't care—it's like Scheerbart!—though I could hear his publisher groaning in protest all the way from Chicago.

"Sure, I'll sign this," I said. I fished a pen out of my pocket along with a crumpled buck.

"You needn't actually give me the dollar," he said, sheepishly, but I insisted; whatever the project was, I wanted to be part of it. I pressed the buck into his hand. He looked at it, almost regretfully, then brusquely shoved it in his pocket like an accursed thing.

"Relax, I can spare it," I said, as I signed the contract. "So what's this project?"

"I'll play it for you," he said, waving his hands in the air like a sorcerer. At this, the theremin whirred to life, like a ghost in a flying saucer. His command of the theremin—for he is surely, I thought, among the foremost thereminists of our day—was so impressive it took me several moments to notice his own instrument was still tucked away in the corner, the amp almost ostentatiously unplugged. It was like he was playing the room, or the room had been wired for theremin.

As Andrew conducted, or should I say *coaxed*, the disembodied sounds from the walls, I looked at the contract I'd signed, which I was still holding. I watched almost in a trance as certain words on the page deformed themselves and reformed to the rhythm of his movement. In due course the contract read:

On this 7th day of October, in the earth year 20**, the undersigned purchaser, Garrett Caples, agrees to purchase the title *PROSES* from its coiner, Nebulon the Categorical, in exchange for the poet's brain.

Garrett Caples, Poet

Nebulon the Categorical

I looked up at Andrew.

"Who the fuck is Nebulon?"

"It is I," he said, "Nebulon, the Categorical!"

He pressed his fingers against the patch of tiny white scars on his chin. His face seemed to split in two, as though it were being unzipped. The two halves fell away, revealing another face beneath that looked more or less identical to Andrew Joron, though noticeably greener.

"Behold!" he said. "Nebulon the Categorical!" He aimed his finger at the furiously barking Tater, who similarly seemed to unzip before my eyes. His skin fell away, as though a husk, disclosing a marginally smaller and greener Tater. He stopped barking and regarded me with what seemed like calculating appraisal.

"Does Rose know about this?" I demanded.

Even in the guise of Nebulon, Andrew looked suddenly abashed.

"No," he admitted.

"I didn't think so!"

"Silence, human!"

"You can't *silence, human* me!" I said.

But it was too late. Nebulon, for it was he, Andrew Joron no longer, waved his hands, and through the ensuing whirr of theremin a large jar materialized on his desk, bearing an ornate label inscribed with the name Kevin Killian, which had been crossed out, while my own name was hastily scrawled above it. Nebulon pointed at the jar, which began to fill with a clear but viscous liquid, like a translucent green pulque. Then, in what might have been the last glimpse of whatever part of his being was Andrew Joron, Nebulon frowned as he affixed a tiny pair of googly eyes to the label. The process seemed to tax his manual dexterity, as though it had deteriorated from excessive reliance on his thereminic powers.

I started to think I should I leave, but before I could move, Nebulon waved his arms and my ears filled with the most unearthly squall, piercing my temples and sinuses, and I thought I'd go deaf or mad if it didn't immediately stop. But it did stop, or rather everything went dark and silent for the next several moments. I couldn't feel my body, but I had a sensation of falling, then gradually my vision returned, blurrily at first until several moments more had passed, and the atmosphere around me appeared to settle into place.

I could see the room, but at a vastly different angle. Nebulon was there, stooping over a prone body that I recognized as my own. The top of my head had been sheared clean off and was floating to one side, yet remarkably no visible gore resulted from this state of affairs. Nebulon waved his arms once again, and my body stood, as though of its own accord, and even at my weird angle of observation I could tell—my brain was gone!

Nebulon reached across my field of vision and grabbed a biscuit from Tater's tin, which was next to me on the desk. He looked down at me, then tossed the biscuit over his shoulder and into my head, where it landed with a thud like a Tootsie Roll dropped in a plastic jack-o'-lantern.

"Excessive reliance on his thereminic powers!" he sneered. He gestured grandly and the sheared-off portion of my head reattached itself to the rest. I watched in horror as Nebulon and my brainless body engaged in a bit of small talk before he sent it out of the mancave and into the night. Nebulon closed the door, and turned to me.

"As for you..." he said. He lifted me off the desk and carried me over to the wall; where bookshelves and LPs once stood were now simply rows of shelves of brains sealed inside labeled jars, some of which were also adorned with googly eyes, which seemed to follow our movements with interest. There was a gap in one of the rows of jars—next to a jar labeled "Brian Lucas"—into which Nebulon carefully set my own. Brian rolled his eyes, and I could somehow feel him say, "It's worse than when he was in Cloud Shepherd!"

I squinted my googly eyes and could just make out some of the names inscribed on the rows of jars on the opposite wall. Gerard de Nerval, Charles Baudelaire, Comte de Lautréamont, Clark Ashton Smith, Thomas Lovell Beddoes, Friedrich Schiller, on and on, a bewildering array of poets from a period spanning hundreds of years. There were even some of our more recent friends, Barbara Guest, Gustav Sobin, Philip Lamantia. There were other jars, like mine or Brian's, labeled with the names of still-living poets, but I don't wish to say whose, for fear of prejudicing reception of their work.

The other poet brains and I can communicate to some degree through our thoughts, and Brian and I sometimes discuss what Nebulon's objectives could be. That he's clearly in the midst of a lengthy mission gathering poet brains is undeniable, but what could be the end of this activity? Nebulon doesn't confide in us; occasionally, he locks himself in the mancave and plays the jars with his distant hand gestures, transforming the entire room into a roiling sea of theremin noise. But otherwise his life as Andrew Joron seemingly continues unabated, as far as I can tell from my vantage on the shelf. Various bandmates come through for rehearsals, Andrew still writes and still plays conventional theremin, and he even receives the occasional visit from my body and whatever alien intelligence he has substituted in for my brain. They seem to have a good time, like we always did, and I admit I'm a little stung by this, though not as much as I am by the fact that I didn't even get my own jar. (Kevin must have died before Nebulon could get ahold of his brain.)

One day my body came by and left behind a book, which Andrew later held up to my jar. The cover said: "*PROSES /* Garrett Caples." He opened the book to the first page, which read:

THE THEREMINIST

I am seven years older than Andrew Joron was when we first met some 25 years ago. In that time, I have grown old, fat, ridiculous, while Andrew—I won't say looks *the same*—he certainly looks older—but he looks *just as well* as he did at age 40. . . .

I stopped reading; I already knew how it ends.

"You don't," Nebulon said.

STEP FOOT

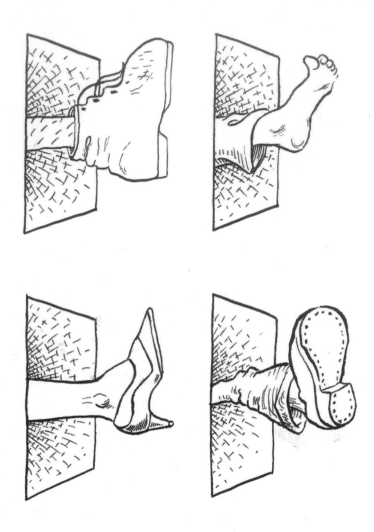

". . . a boot kicking the man out the door . . ."

for **Kit Schluter**

"And stay out!"

It was just like the cartoons: two hands and a boot kicking the man out the door and headlong across the sidewalk into the gutter, where he landed with a sickening thud. The door slammed theatrically. The man lay in a heap groaning, as I hurried to his side to help him, unsteadily, to his feet.

The man had scraped his chin and forehead on the sidewalk. I took the handkerchief from the breast pocket of his dingy suit and dabbed at the oozing wounds. He looked dazed, though his face would have looked haggard at the best times.

"What happened?" I asked. His gaze suddenly snapped into focus.

"Step foot!" he cried. "Step foot!"

The man was clearly mad.

"It's OK," I said, drawing him along by the elbow. "Lemme buy you a coffee."

We entered a nearby Starbucks. The manager was on us in a flash.

"Not you!" she said, glaring at him. "Not today!"

It was worse than I thought. I led him to the Starbucks across the street. Here he was unknown. I deposited him at a table and bought us a couple coffees. When I returned he was blotting the scrape on his forehead with his handkerchief. He clutched the coffee cup eagerly, almost crushing it as he drank with a trembling hand.

"What happened?"

"Step foot!" he nearly shouted. Then, lowering his voice and whispering bitterly: "Step foot!" He ran his fingers through his hair.

"What do you mean, 'step foot'?"

"Exactly!" the man cried, his eyes shining in triumph. "What does it mean? Not a goddamn thing!" This again almost shouted, but the man grew suddenly aware of his surroundings, and looked around, afraid of attracting attention. Restraining himself with an effort, he hissed out: "Not a goddamn thing."

He took a gulp of coffee and seemed to settle down.

"I was once," he began, "like you—"

"I doubt it," I said, though I quickly sensed this wasn't a dialog.

"—a productive member of society, with a job, no, a career,

successful even, in my own way. Making it! Sure, I bemoaned the increasing vulgarity of both language and manners, but I didn't kid myself, I was part of it too. It's just life now, end of story, and not some Argentine novella type story, either."

"Christ, is this a millenni—"

"Idioms got mangled, turned into initials, became little pictures, then little pictures that moved. I LOL'd it up with the best of them. Had to; life was faster and that's what it took to keep up.

"Then one day I noticed this phrase, *step foot*. It was in some trashy publication, like *Hollywood Life*, some celebrity gossip thing I read online at work, and I probably thought, 'This simpleton doesn't know how to write,' because the phrase is *set foot*, and only a TV-recapping fuckwitted fool of a *Hollywood Life* writer could possibly imagine the phrase was *step foot*. Step *foot*? As opposed to what: Step *head*? Step *hand*? You *set foot* in a place. Or you *step* into, on, over, wherever, it doesn't matter, step *means* you use your fucking foot, you fucking fuckwit!

"Normally, such evidence of decayed literacy would only cause me fleeting annoyance, and I would move on with my day, but this was different. There was something positively revolting about the redundancy. And I no sooner had noticed the phrase than I began to see it—not everywhere at first, but more like a rash gradually spreading over the course of several years. But each time I encountered it, in increasingly respectable publications, *The Atlantic*, let's say, or *Harper's Bazaar*, my almost physical revulsion grew. I started making involuntary noises, audible, I was sure, outside my cubicle and definitely noticed on the subway. I had to stop reading my phone in public lest people think I'm crazy, but then not being on your phone makes people think you're crazy.

"The phrase spread like an insidious disease that only I could detect, while my own symptoms grew increasingly alarming. Then one day at work, at the very end of an article about Miami's Little Havana in the *New York Times*, I read: 'it has a lot to offer travelers looking to experience Cuban culture without having to step foot off the lower 48.' Now I'd encountered the phrase in the *Times* before, but as reported dialog—Marco Rubio, for example, debating Donald Trump in the Republican primary and vowing to end DACA 'as soon as I step foot into the Oval Office'—and granted this was only in the travel section, but seeing the phrase uninflected in 9-pt. Gray Lady provoked a violent spasm within me. I felt my nostrils flare, and air filled my lungs until I thought my chest would burst. My head was thrown back, my mouth opened, and out came the most hideous scream I had ever heard, morbid and wrenching, like the howls of a thousand Nosferatus caught outside at sunrise and bursting into putrid flames. A scream of terror and death.

"I immediately lost consciousness, only to awaken some time later in a hospital room, where a doctor was frowning over my chart. *Afraid we don't know what happened, never heard anything like it, some sort of episode*, all the useless verbiage of a man of science confounded by phenomena blathered from his mouth, but I knew what had happened, or at least what made it happen. I had crossed some sort of toxic threshold with the phrase *step foot*. I knew I could never lay eyes on it again, or else I would fall victim to its dreaded physical side effects.

"But it was impossible! They were understanding at work the second time it happened, but after the third time, I was let go. The scream was worse every time. I was bruising ribs and cracking glass. It's been years of torment since. I have lost four jobs, five wives, six boyfriends, seven apartments, eight teeth, nine therapists! Short of not reading at all, I can't avoid the phrase. It forces itself on me. I can't make myself forget how to read!"

"Horseshit!" I said.

The man was so startled he crushed his cup altogether.

"What?" he rasped.

"It's a common mistake," I said, pulling up the *Times* on my phone and popping "step foot" into the search. "The phrase *step foot* has appeared in the *New York Times* . . . 153 times. Look." I held out my phone but it was like I'd offered Dracula a basket of garlic fries. He recoiled in horror.

"Well, trust me; it's one fifty-three. It's an old mistake too. All the way back to . . ." I sorted the results. ". . . 1858, it seems."

The man looked at me with barely restrained hate. His neck veins bulged.

"Reported!" he cried. He looked around again, and hissed in a lower voice. "The 1858 reference is language reported over telegraph from Syracuse of the Liberty Party platform protesting the Fugitive Slave Act."

I looked at my phone. He was right!

"You don't think I checked, imbecile, back when I could stand to?"

"Fine," I said, "1885 then":

To these charges the electric wires which are to explode the mine are attached, and during the operation of putting them in place and thereafter until the time of their designated use no person other than the Government officers and workmen will be allowed to step foot within the limits of the Flood Rock excavation.

"That's the reporter," I said, "not the reported."

He glared at me.

"It's just a harmless mistake," I said. "Christ, even FDR says it in a radio address in 1944."

"He couldn't walk!" the man almost shouted.

"He could talk," I said.

Suddenly, the anger left him; he sighed, and held his head in his hands.

"How many times," he asked, "does *step foot* appear in the *Times* prior to 1989?"

I counted: "Twenty-seven."

"Twenty seven times. Of those, three are accidental juxtapositions, like the reference to a 'two-step foot rest' in 1947, and one is a 1913 rerun of a 1903 puff piece about men at ladies' lunchrooms. So it's really 23 times, in the first 137 years of the *New York Times*."

"What happened in '89? Taylor Swift?"

That aforementioned look of barely restrained hate flashed across his face before he sighed wearily.

"Historians will one day study why the Reagan Era was strangely immune to the ravages of the phrase, but the fact remains that *step foot* disappears from the paper between 1980 and 1989. Since then, the phrase has appeared 126 times." He pounded his fist on the table. "It's only been 30 years!"

This last outburst definitely turned a few heads in our direction, but the man didn't seem to notice.

"It's killing me!" he hissed.

I took a long slow slug of coffee and switched from the *Times* to my Notes app. I started typing as furiously as I could using just my thumbs.

"Look," I said, "I'm a poet; you just need a poem to fix you up. Here..."

I offered my phone again. After a moment's hesitation, he reached for it, still eyeing me warily.

On my Notes app, I'd thumbed out the following bit of doggerel:

> staring down
> the passage of time
> everyone knows
> painful phrases

> forgetting the city
> of language is subject
> only to the rule of
> temporary endurance

He frowned, the way most people do when they read a poem.
"I don't get it," he said, poring over the screen.
"It's an acrostic," I said.

I'm uncertain how long I was unconscious. When I awoke, I
was in a hospital room, where a doctor was frowning over my
chart.

"Never seen anything like it," she said. Her voice sounded
faint, like she was speaking behind a pane of glass, or I'd just
attended a rock concert. I closed my eyes and tried to remember what had happened. I had a fleeting image in my
mind of the man looking at me in an agony of fear as his
mouth dropped open. Then it all went black.

Over the next several days as my hearing returned to normal, through conversations with doctors, nurses, and a pair
of homicide detectives, I pieced together what happened.
The man had had another episode, a final episode. A large
sonic boom had been recorded in Midtown Manhattan. The

windows of the Starbucks had shattered, people were hurt, and the man himself had been almost wholly incinerated, leaving behind a few charred remains and a bloody handkerchief. My phone had been reduced to ashes, so my role in the incident remained mercifully concealed. I professed to be as shocked as everyone. *Never seen him before, just a poor ol' crazy guy I bought a cup of coffee*, that sort of thing. The detectives believed me. They did ask, however, about the search recorded on my nytimes.com account not long before the disaster.

"Just working on a poem," I said.

"Some poem," one of them said.

I wasn't a suspect. But the episode weighed no less heavily on my thoughts. It made no sense. As I walked the streets, recovering from the ordeal, I found myself still arguing with the man.

"But *footstep* is a word," I said.

"That's to distinguish *step* from *stair*, or *measure*. That makes sense!" he said.

It was useless, but I couldn't make myself stop.

One night, after hours of aimless walking, I found myself walking down 6th Avenue. I stopped at the corner of West 48th, and stood in a small crowd, waiting for the light to change. I closed my eyes, and tried to concentrate on breathing, surrounded by a hive of a million urban noises. When I heard the light change, I opened my eyes.

It was there floating across my field of vision in lurid red letters, on the news ticker on the side of the News Corp. Building:

Trump is first sitting US president to step foot in North Korea

I fell to my knees in the crosswalk. I felt my nostrils flare and the air rushed into my lungs so quickly I thought my ribs would break. I threw back my head and howled.

HECTOR NICE

". . . which I suspected was mostly brandy."

His name was Nice, Hector Nice—pronounced like the city —which was funny both because he was nice in an unctuous, mannered way, and because he was anything but, due to a combination of limited ability and limitless ambition that manifested itself in ruthless devotion to his career. This ruthlessness could be gauged by the circumstances of the time. For it had been a rough year, culminating in a pair of rough months. The entire country had been shut down since March due to a pandemic, and the pandemic was only getting worse. Millions were unemployed, and hundreds of thousands were routinely taking to the streets to protest the systemic oppression of people of color. The presidential election had taken place at the beginning of November, but the losing incumbent—whose incompetent response to the pandemic had caused untold loss of life—refused to concede, throwing the country into crisis with baseless conspiracy theories that the election had been stolen. The volatile situation finally reached a convulsion when the president sicced a group of his armed supporters on the legislature as it attempted to certify his opponent's victory. This was unprecedented not simply in my own experience and lifetime but in the history of the country, period. Each day brought fresh uncertainty that overwhelmed any sense of relief brought on by the election's outcome, and we were literally counting the moments until the change of administration, which would hopefully put an end to this madness.

And to what pursuit had Hector Nice, poet, professor, unacknowledged legislator of men—he once told me he wanted be read by doctors! lawyers!—to what civic-minded purpose had he dedicated himself lo these past two months, during which the principles of our nation's governance, indeed our fundamental beliefs about our society, were shaken to their very core? To my torment!

And worse yet, my torment was a matter not merely of indifference but more like ignorance on the part of Hector Nice, for he was motivated by no animosity towards me, but rather by an intensity of self-absorption and self-regard that made it impossible for him to imagine what it's like for an editor to receive *the same manuscript 14 times over the course of a two-month period*, against the cataclysmic backdrop I've painted above. That's like once every four days, though there was no pattern to the arrivals, simply a drearily repeated "THIS version is MUCH better" in every email the manuscript was attached to. Once I got two in one day, but he took the holidays off like a normal person, so I'd get a string of days where there were no emails, and I'd forget it was even happening. Then boom: two in two days. I was in the blackest depression—the short winter days were killing me—I was fed up with lockdown, and I was more than a little concerned by the spasms of authoritarianism in the administration's death throes. "THIS version is MUCH better" was exactly the type of provocation that could send the increasingly fragile edifice of my sanity tumbling to the ground.

And yet it was my own fault; he'd set an obvious trap, and I walked right into it. I blame the lockdown; my instincts were rusty. For a good decade I'd been fencing with Hector Nice, successfully parrying his attempts to thrust himself onto the list at Verdoux Books, a prestigious though impoverished publisher, attached to a bookstore, specializing in political tracts of a left-leaning nature and, of course, even worse-selling, poetry. I had stumbled into an editorial situation there, precarious and ill-paid, but when you've been laboring so long as a poet and person of letters, anything is a step up from the nothing you're accustomed to, so I made it work, even as I had to freelance in my off hours to make ends meet. There was just no money in poetry these days, but Verdoux was founded on poetry—*GOOF* by Philip Whalen has sold almost two million copies—and there was no way the press could not publish poetry, certainly not while Old Man Verdoux was still alive. My editorial remit was largely devoted to the problem of how to publish poetry without losing a ton of money. And one of the many ways I went about fulfilling this brief was by not publishing Hector Nice.

Mind you, I had nothing against him personally; in fact, I considered him a friend of sorts. I even thought he was a half-decent poet, which is way further than I permit myself to think about most people I meet under that dubious rubric. I could kill an hour now and again walking around the lake and chatting with him about poetry. But he was a "professional poet," a department chair at some college that didn't know any better, published by White Hoof Books, a prestigious and well-heeled press largely funded by grants. I was convinced no one bought his books. No one I knew ever came to me all hepped up on some Hector Nice. But more important was the principle of thing. He had a nice job in a nice city and was published by a nice press. It was more than he had any right to, and I knew many poets who would give a great deal for even one of those things.

But Hector Nice wanted more, including publication by

the publisher of *GOOF*, and my goal was always to keep him from submitting anything so as to not have to say outright that I wouldn't publish him. To preserve cordiality. Every now and then I was summoned for a walk around the lake, and we would engage in oblique and diplomatic discourse on the matter, like a couple of characters from *The Tale of Genji*, him sounding me out on the state of affairs at the press and the poetry we were thinking about publishing, me extolling the virtues of a press like White Hoof. "I wish *we* could take on poets like White Hoof does," I'd say, "but we can't afford to. We can give a poet usually one book at the most. It's way better for a poet at White Hoof, where they stick with their authors." That type of thing. I laid it on thick and impenetrable, and gradually the crisis would pass, and I'd spend the rest of the walk listening to the problems of a poet with a nice job in a nice city who was published by a nice press, and the problems were endless because nothing was ever enough for Hector Nice, because his ambition was primarily directed toward his "career" as opposed to his poetry. I would usually be so relieved at successfully avoiding a submission that his subsequent litany of self-aggrandizement and self-pity was positively bracing, and I would hum or cluck sympathetically as the rhythms of his frustrations dictated.

Having engaged in such evasive combat for years, I don't know how I could have been such a fool as to set foot in his snare, which came in the form of an email, on November 2, the day before the election.

> Dearest Claude:
>
> How are you doing, etc.? I've written a new book and I was hoping you would read the MS. May I send it to you?
>
> Yours,
> Hector

Now I know what you're thinking; this is a transparent attempt to submit a manuscript and how could an editor of any years' standing possibly fall for so ill-concealed a ruse? (As if making that mistake were inherently less plausible than someone submitting the same manuscript 14 times in two months!) But recall too I'm a poet as well as an editor, and in my preoccupation with the then-impending election, I assumed I was being consulted here as a fellow practitioner, because this too was a thing with Hector Nice. Under the flattering guise of consultation, he would ensure that dozens of poets of all manner of description read his upcoming book. I'd done this before, as had other poets I knew. He paid me to proofread one once, when I was young and broke. And despite the fact that, as an editor, I have more manuscripts piled up than I can conceivably get to, even I could find the time to run through a manuscript of Hector Nice. For all Hector Nice manuscripts were roughly the same: about 52 pages and a 1,200-word word count; a suite or two of poems where the title would be strewn two or three times down the page, with little flecks of barely there drifting beneath them. Don't get me wrong, he could actually put together decent lines of poetry, but he doled them out with the strictest economy. A new Hector Nice book was maybe an every-five-years' affair, and I could easily spare the 20 minutes or so it would take me to read one at so indolent a rate of production, if it meant keeping the peace. And too, he already had a publisher. So, with a rashness I would soon regret, I immediately wrote back, *Sure, I'd be happy to read it!*

Like lightning, he pressed his point home and I was cut to the quick, if either of those are fencing metaphors. The manuscript immediately materialized in my inbox, accompanied by the following note:

Beloved Claude:

Here is the new manuscript. Will you publish it?

Love,
Hector

Fucking hell! I ejaculated. During the pandemic, I was, of course, working at home, so I quickly shut down my computer, staggered to my bed as though wounded, and collapsed upon it, writhing in agony. How could I have been so careless? Of course, it was a submission! I was a fool! Over a decade of tactical maneuvers, wasted! I indulged in such self-recriminations for several minutes, before pulling myself together, and taking a draught from my bedside bottle of Dr. Johnson's Fortifying Tonic for Editors, which I ordered from an ad in the back of *Publishers Weekly* and which I suspected was mostly brandy. I reassured myself; it was the day before the election. I was distracted, vulnerable. My ability to read my fellow man had atrophied due to the prolonged isolation of the pandemic.

Having settled my nerves, I returned to my desk and rebooted my machine. There was nothing for it except to tell him outright I couldn't publish him. Letting the submission sit would only exacerbate an already intolerable situation, and I'd lost precious minutes writhing. With a heavy heart I logged onto my email, and tapped out the following:

Dear Hector:

I'm sorry, old friend, but I'm not allowed to take on anything at Verdoux right now, due to the pandemic. The organization is hemorrhaging money, and we're fighting for survival. But I am still happy to read your new manuscript. Aren't you publishing with White Hoof anymore?

Sincerely,
Claude

Weaselly? Yes! But I was a broken man. I needed time to heal and time was what I didn't have if I wanted to turn this touché into a ceding parry before he ran me through. And the strategy, it seemed, succeeded; that evening, I received a long, magnanimous note commiserating with me about the evils of the pandemic, inquiring solicitously about Verdoux, and ruing the evils of the present administration. My question about White Hoof remained unaddressed, but the anticipated crisis had been averted, so much so I was inspired to send my own magnanimous follow up, thanking him for his understanding and assuring him I would read his new manuscript as soon as time permitted. I even downloaded the attachment. Inwardly, I chastised myself for my unreasonable fears; poets could accept a kind refusal once in a while, I needn't be so circumspect in my handling of them. I spent that day in an orgy of editorial activity, polishing off work on a manuscript from a recently deceased poet with much pleasure, as I find the deceased are, with some exceptions, easier to work with. I felt like a schoolboy on holiday, a schoolboy who still had to finish his homework, true, but one who found the work enjoyable divorced from the more sordid aspects of school attendance. For me, the sun that day set on a world with which all was fleetingly right, tinted by the warm glow of Dr. Johnson's Fortifying Tonic for Editors.

Of course, nothing was right with the world, and the next day, after months of unrest, economic freefall, and pandemic deaths on a gruesome scale, the election took place. I'd already voted by mail weeks earlier, so I fired up my computer, prepared to go to work as usual and spend the day refreshing my browser like the rest of the country while we awaited the election results. You will appreciate, therefore, my consternation when I logged into my email, only to find another message from Hector Nice, one reading simply "THIS version is MUCH better," with a new iteration of the manuscript attached. A feeling of dread crept over me, even as I assured myself there was nothing here to dread. Hadn't we all sent a manuscript out, only to notice some niggling little detail hitherto overlooked in the face of more urgent structural issues whose address couldn't be postponed? Only when the main pieces had been slotted into the manuscript in the correct order could those more subtle but nonetheless crucial issues command the author's attention. A hideous blunder could sail right past you, if you were in a hurry. And yet, these reflections didn't quite set me at ease. Why, I wondered, had he reintroduced the topic of submitting to Verdoux after it had lain dormant for a few years by now? That is, why, besides the profound state of discontent over his career that Hector Nice perpetually dwelt in? His evasion of my inquiries on the subject of White Hoof suddenly cast an ominous light on the affair; had there been a rupture? I chose not to reply to the email for the time being, and settled down to work, uneasily, the questions gnawing at the back of my mind.

But gradually, the nailbiting details of the election, and the vote tallies trickling in from those few states whose results would decide it, crowded out my mundane, professional concerns. And the uncertainty stretched on for days, until the contest was finally decided, decisively, against the incompetent and evil incumbent. Yet even then, the relief was exceedingly brief, for the president had already begun to weave his own counternarrative of how the election had been stolen from him by some amorphous means of fraud perpetuated by the other party. The assertion was childish, but so were the president's supporters, so it spoke to them like gospel.

This new form of chaos took hold of the nation's attention, and was all the more sinister as the election hadn't been *fully* decided. The president had lost, true, but due to the arcana of local election laws, one state would hold a runoff election, scheduled for January, to determine whether his party retained control of the legislature, or whether the new president-elect's party would gain the upper hand and so facilitate a new agenda. The brief euphoria of seeing the president voted out of office gave way to an additional two months of agony as we waited to learn the country's fate.

The day the election was called against the president, a Saturday, I went to the mailbox, to find, among the bills and circulars, the latest issue of *Publishers Weekly*. I was forced to subscribe to the print edition, so I could continue to order my supply of Dr. Johnson's Fortifying Tonic for Editors. They didn't advertise online and their postal address seemed to change with an irritating frequency. As I leafed through the magazine, my eye caught a glimpse of a headline, and I flipped back a few pages to find it. There it was: "Boating Accident Claims White Hoof Head." "O. A. Tatlock is out at White Hoof," the item began, "as the celebrated publisher/editor fell from the deck of a Madeline Island Ferry boat into the icy waters of Lake Superior below on October 20." Tatlock gone! Just like that, with no succession plan! A nation-wide search for a suitable replacement was already under-way. Of course! Tatlock had handled Hector Nice's books personally. If Tatlock was out at White Hoof, Hector Nice probably was too. It happens all the time in publishing; an editor leaves a press and suddenly doors once propped open invitingly to a number of poets are violently slammed shut without so much as a by-your-leave. It took no huge leap of imagination to suppose the rest of the staff at White Hoof thought Hector Nice was an insufferable bastard, and let's face it, even a well-heeled press could do with a little belt-tightening here and there. No doubt the staff would take the opportunity of Tatlock's demise to unload a number of poets who were both a pain in the ass and not very remunerative.

That day I received the manuscript in my inbox twice, once in the morning, once in the late afternoon. "THIS ver sion is MUCH better," I was assured both times.

I didn't reply. I figured absolute radio silence would get the message across, and he'd eventually abandon this puerile campaign. But I figured wrong. Every few days, when I least expected it, a new copy of the manuscript, accompanied by that drear falsehood of its superiority to the previous iteration, would arrive in my inbox, jarring on my perpetually keyed up nerves like I'd stepped on a rake. It was beyond reason and below dignity. But it was a fact, one that recurred with desperate frequency. Finally, when I could bear it no longer, I added his email address to my junk filter. This brought some peace, but it was a peace compromised by tension. Every now and then I would peek into the junk folder to see when his most recent email had arrived. But I didn't have leisure to devote to the burgeoning if virtual stack of manuscripts. I had work to do, and my waking moments were otherwise taken up by political concerns. The outgoing president continued to fan the flames of his misinformation campaign about the election being stolen, but all of his attempts to interrupt the process of certifying his opponent's victory were laughably ineffective, while his court challenges were dismissed with scathing commentary by judges, some of whom he himself had appointed. It was exhausting even to follow in the news.

The one thing the president did succeed in accomplishing was whipping his most die-hard supporters into seditious frenzy, resulting in roving bands of bozos besieging state capitols and clashing with cops and counterdemonstrators. It was a sideshow, of course, with little chance of affecting the upcoming change of administrations, so I ignored it as best I could while I obsessed over the runoff campaigns that would determine which party controlled the legislature. My mood and outlook steadily darkened with the late afternoon sky as we neared the solstice. Thanksgiving came and went, then the consumerist nightmare of Christmas lurched our way, unmitigated by any pretense of real holiday cheer given the lack of opportunity to get together with family and friends due to the pandemic. It was all pleas to buy things in the middle of the biggest economic crisis since the Great Depression. Finally, the holidays were over, and the daylight almost imperceptibly began to lengthen. I felt like hell, but I also began to feel the lightest stirrings of optimism within my soul.

The runoff was held on January 5, the first Tuesday of the year, but the results were too close to call by the time I went to sleep that night. When I awoke the next morning, and to my great relief, the president-elect's party had emerged victorious, but any feelings of elation that turn of events raised were immediately lowered as the incumbent goaded a crowd of his supporters into attacking the Capitol Building as the legislature attempted to certify the results of the November election. I'm no great patriot but you don't have to be a great patriot to be furious at the spectacle of armed white supremacists attempting to thwart the result of an election you voted in. It's hard not to take personally, just as it was hard not to take personally the torment incidental to his ambition that Hector Nice inflicted on me with his ruthless campaign of alleged revision and continual resubmission.

The afternoon of the day after this failed insurrection took place, I checked my junk folder; a new version of the manuscript had arrived, along with a new "THIS version is MUCH better." I sorted the folder by sender, selected all the Hector Nice emails, and made them their own new folder. I tallied up the number of times he'd sent the manuscript: 14. Something about the total seemed to send me over the edge, and I decided this had to stop. I hit reply to the most recent email, fully intending to tell Hector Nice what a self-obsessed creep he was, spamming me with his manuscript at a time like this. Instead, I found myself typing:

Dear Hector:

I finally had a chance to read your manuscript. It's brilliant! Meet me at the lake tonight by the gazebo at 7 so we can discuss it.

Sincerely,
Claude

What the hell was I thinking? I wondered as I found myself driving over to Verdoux Books. But I felt a strange passivity, like I was sitting somewhere watching someone else park, mask up, and head down the hill to the bookstore. I said hi to various friends working at the sparsely patronized retail space behind various plexiglass shields. I ran upstairs to the office. It was locked, as most of the publishing staff was working from home these days, but I had a key. I let myself in and fired up one of the computers. While it booted, I grabbed a sheet of Verdoux Books letterhead and placed it in the office printer. Then I rummaged around on the computer for a minute until I found one of our standard poetry contracts, which I printed so that the first page appeared on our letterhead. I checked my email, and as anticipated, Hector Nice had confirmed our appointment mere minutes after I sent it. I shut everything down, grabbed the contract from the printer, and locked the office back up. I made one more round through the store to say hi to some colleagues, then headed back up the hill to my car.

It was only around 5 but the sky was rapidly blackening the way it did so early at that time of year, and it would be dark as midnight well before I succeeded in crossing the bridge, by the time I found myself parking at the lake, on the opposite side from the tiny beach where the gazebo was located, it was just shy of 6 p.m. More than enough time for an unhurried stroll along the banks; though it was dark the lake was surrounded by what was referred to locally as "the Necklace" of lights, consisting of strings of small lightbulbs linking each lamppost to the next, so I could watch the egrets and herons stalking the shallows for prey. At length, I reached the tiny beach near the gazebo, where the Canada geese always congregated at night, some on shore, some drifting semiconscious in the water. Otherwise, the area seemed to be deserted, what with the darkness, the cold, and the pandemic. I stood under a lamppost where I'd be visible from any angle of approach and fingered the pages of the blank contract nervously. I took a pull from my travel-size bottle of Dr. Johnson's Fortifying Tonic for Editors. I waited.

Not long after 7 I saw a dark form emerge from a path behind some trees and trudge in my direction. Even before I could make out any features, I could tell it was Hector Nice by the shambling gait and the air of distracted hurry surrounding him like a cloud. He was always clean but disheveled, like he'd fallen through a hedge en route to his destination. He saluted me as he approached with a raised hand and a hale shout of "Claude!" I had to time my maneuvers perfectly, so I called out "Hector!" and brandished the document so the lamplight glinted off the gilded lettering of the Verdoux Books letterhead. This caught his eye as he advanced for a handshake and I let the pages slip from my fingers as if by accident, as a light breeze blew and carried them into the lake. "Your contract!" I shouted, as though dismayed. I saw his eyes widen in horror as he took in my words and with an astonishing alacrity for one so lumbering, and an admirable lack of hesitation at the decisive moment for action, he dove headlong after the fluttering pages and even managed to catch one as he splattered against the fetid muck offshore with a sound like a mallet hitting a wall of fudge.

I was on him at once. The water was only a few inches deep, rather less than I had imagined, so I was forced to push his head down to keep his face submerged, with the rest of my weight on his back so he couldn't get up. He flailed about ineffectually but with great persistence, while angry geese flapped around us, protesting vocally, and it felt like several minutes had passed before his limbs stopped struggling and his body went limp. Still I held on, making sure he was well and truly gone. Finally, I relaxed my grip and looked around. No witnesses, as far as I could tell, save for the Canada geese. I thought about dragging the body into deeper water and gathering the pages of the contract, but instead left everything where it was and squelched back to my car, carrying my shoes. There was no way I wasn't going to be caught, so why bother? I returned home, threw my clothes in the wash, wrote some overdue catalog copy, and went to bed that night a condemned man.

The next morning, I showered and dressed as soon as I got up, which I assure you was never my habit, pandemic or no. I fully expected the police to arrive at any moment to take me away and hoped to cut a more sympathetic figure than robe and underpants might afford. The emails, the contract, it was all too obvious, and I may as well have turned myself in immediately. I cracked the door so they wouldn't have to break it down, assuming I was a dangerous killer who needed to be taken unawares. I looked around the apartment with a certain amount of weltschmerz, imagining I might never see it again, yet I felt remarkably at peace with my actions, more peaceful, in fact, than at any moment since the pandemic began. I tried to fix the apartment's details in my memory. Then I got bored and logged on, to see whether my manhunt was underway, and if so, what was taking so long.

There it was, at the top of Google News: "Lakeside Killer Dead; Two More Victims Found." Alongside this headline was a photograph of a local realtor that looked as if it'd been cropped from a bus-bench ad and what I instantly recognized as Hector Nice's standard publicity headshot. I read on in disbelief. Police had shot and killed the notorious Lakeside Killer, who'd been terrorizing the district for months in what authorities believe was the deadliest part of a recent crimewave instigated by the economic effects of the pandemic, during which time so many local businesses had shuttered. He'd been rifling through the pockets of his second victim of the night, poet and professor Hector Nice, in the shallow waters near the gazebo at the lake, and taken down in a hail of gunfire from officers responding to the discovery of his first victim, ReMax 2014 Realtor of the Year Jennelle Booker, among a nearby stand of trees. It was the first time, police believed, that the killer had struck twice in one night.

This unlooked-for coincidence, while welcome, and—let's face it—still more plausible than a poet sending an editor an already-turned-down manuscript 14 times over the course of two months, was not without its complications for me personally, due to the presence of the contract at the scene of the crime and the emails concerning our rendezvous. I had to testify at the inquest. I had to explain to my boss at Verdoux what I was doing bringing Hector Nice a contract during the night, so I made up an excuse, that I was just sharing some insider knowledge he could compare with the terms offered by White Hoof. I had to read at the memorial reading, fortunately over Zoom due to the pandemic, so I was able to get through it with a handle of Dr. Johnson's Fortifying Tonic for Editors concealed off camera. I had to listen to poets who I knew for a fact thought Hector Nice was the most obnoxious person they knew give the most fulsome eulogies for his life and his talent. At some point, I think I even spoke to the *New York Times* about him, where I treaded a fine line between praising him enough to maintain my cover and deflecting any expectations that Verdoux was going to publish him. I half-expected White Hoof to step in and announce it would publish what now had to be considered his final book, though I heard precious little on that front. Even my boss began to wonder aloud whether or not Verdoux should publish Hector Nice, as a gesture to help the poetry community heal from the tragedy. I told her we should wait to see what White Hoof did. He was, after all, their poet.

By the time of the memorial, the nation was breathing a collective sigh of relief, as power was finally transferred from the incumbent's administration to the new one. But this long-dreamt-of development brought me little sense of peace in the end, for the following day, I received an email from Hector Nice. Impossible! you say, which is pretty much what I said, though my phrasing was more akin to *what the fuck?!?*

But there it was—in my regular inbox rather than my junk folder, although I hadn't changed the setting—complete with that day's date, the usual "THIS version is MUCH better" within, and the manuscript attached. How could this be? Had he been spamming me this whole time with an automatic message, set to some complex algorithm that prevented me from discerning the pattern of its arrival? Had his ambition somehow survived his death? I deleted the message, though I found myself unable to focus on my work thereafter and soon shut everything down and took to my bed. There was precious little left in my bedside bottle of Dr. Johnson's Fortifying Tonic for Editors but I drank it off in one gulp and reached for the latest issue of *Publishers Weekly*. I paged past Ben Lerner's "Hector Nice: An Appreciation," past a full-page ad from White Hoof flogging their back catalog of Hector Nice books, past a call for submissions to the upcoming Hector Nice issue of the *Chicago Review*, frantically seeking the usual ad, but for some reason I couldn't find it. I started again, slowly and more deliberately, licking my fingertips to separate any stuck together pages. Don't tell me the FDA picked this week of all weeks to crack down on Dr. Johnson!

I closed the magazine in a rage. And there it was, taking

up the back cover like an Absolut ad, with a new font and completely redesigned trade dress: JOHNSON'S ENERGY DRINK ... *THIS version is MUCH better!* I screamed in horror and threw the magazine across the room. I drew the sheets over my head and trembled.

The next time I logged onto my email, I found not only a new message and attachment from Hector Nice, but also the previously deleted email from the day before. This time I called the IT department at the college where Hector Nice had taught, explaining that I was still receiving emails from his account. My call was eventually escalated to the head of IT. Impossible, he said, the account had been suspended shortly after the school had been formally notified of his death. I offered to forward him the emails while we were on the phone, but every time I tried, the forward never arrived in his inbox. Following some four or five of my failed attempts, the head of IT began to imply that I was making it up and that doing so was in poor taste, given the circumstances surrounding Professor Nice's death. I could see it was hopeless. I resolved, for the time being, to simply ignore the emails, however unsettling, but they quickly began cluttering my inbox; each time a new one arrived, the older deleted ones somehow returned along with it, and the time spent deleting them lengthened proportionately. After a few weeks, my inbox grew untenable and I was obliged to delete my email address altogether, though I'd been using it professionally for over a decade. I was forced to rely on my verdoux-books.com address, which I seldom used because of its ungainly interface.

The morning after I deleted my email address, I awoke to the sound of my printer printing, which would have been disconcerting at the best of times, but was positively hair-raising now. I ran to my desk to find the printer tray overflowing with output, which spilled from the tray over the desk, and onto the floor. It had to be two or three reams' worth, though my printer can only hold half of one. With trembling fingers, I picked up a sheet and turned it over, then another, then another. Printed once in the center of each page was the sentence I had come to dread above all others in the English language: "THIS version is MUCH better." I unplugged the printer and disconnected it from the computer, and the scrolling of pages ceased. As soon as I retreated back to my bedroom, I heard the printer start printing again. I ran back to my desk. I picked up the unplugged peripheral, opened the front door, and hurled the machine into the street, where it broke in several pieces, pages flying everywhere, to the astonishment of a passing dogwalker and a nanny with a pair of toddlers. I slammed the door shut, locked and bolted it, then retreated back to my bedroom. There would be no work today.

By the following month, it had been arranged for me to take a leave of absence from Verdoux. I needed a complete digital detox, according to my doctor, my therapist, and my psychiatrist; that much was clear, even if I couldn't completely confide in them. Old Man Verdoux even lent me the keys to his cabin in the mountains, though he warned me it was freezing up there at this time of year. I'd have to use the fireplace or the kerosene heater, because there was no electricity or heat. I wasn't the hardy, outdoor-type who would still be alive at 101 like Ol' Verd, but it was exactly what I wanted. I needed to escape all things electronic, for otherwise I feared descending into complete madness. I bought a four-season sleeping bag, a lantern and fuel, a flashlight, candles, a notebook, some pens, and a decent supply of Argentine novellas, which was all I had appetite for reading at this point. I laid in a stock of canned food and some jugs of spring water, and in lieu of my former reliance on Dr. Johnson's Fortifying Tonic for Editors, I went straight for the E&J Brandy. I embarked on the roughly three-hour journey.

By the time the sunlight began to fade in the early evening,

I had the lantern up and running, but I realized I'd never figure out the fireplace that night. I fired up kerosene heater, but it radiated the feeblest circle of warmth, along with a fairly acrid scent. I could see my breath. Shivering in the dark on the bed in my sleeping bag, I realized I had no idea whether it was safe to burn kerosene all night or whether I would die from carbon monoxide. I lay there breathing the acrid air, half-tempted to take my chances. But I soon grew concerned enough to get up in my bag and hop across the room with the lantern to the old toolbox I'd noted earlier. I found a hammer and nails. I hopped over to the side of the cabin opposite the bed and the heater, where there was a small window. I cracked the window open just a slit, then pounded a nail into each side of the frame, so nothing could open it further, or at least, not without waking me up. It was cold as fuck! I dropped the hammer where I stood, then hopped back across the room with the lantern to the bed. I shivered violently for a time then managed to generate enough body heat to just be cold. *This sucks*, I couldn't help thinking.

I sat bolt upright in the bed. The lantern had gone out and the room was pitch black. I must have fallen asleep. As I sat there waiting for my eyes to adjust to the dark, I heard a weird, whispery noise, like the sound of paper sliding across a windowpane. I fumbled around on the bedside table till I found the flashlight. I turned it on and shined it across the room. I froze in horror. There was a huge pile of paper covering the floor beneath the slit of open window, through which pages were sliding in a steady stream, like the output of an industrial photocopier. Trembling from head to toe, I slid out of my sleeping bag and crossed the room. I looked at the pages, many of which had turned over as they slid down the pile; I shined the flashlight on the page closest to my foot. "THIS version is MUCH better," it said. I dropped the flashlight, hearing it break against the floor as I plunged back into darkness. I ran to the door, knocking over some furniture as I fled. I ran through the cold and darkness in just my socks, with rocks and branches lacerating my feet. I ran blindly, for miles it seemed, until my lungs were on fire and I dropped to the ground from exhaustion. As I lay there in a patch of snow, pages began to slowly drift from the sky, like snowflakes, landing on my prone figure. Occasionally, a page would fall over my face and I would reach up and brush it aside, but I was too tired to move. Finally, even this was too difficult, and the pages covered me, blocking my view of the sky.

In the spring, during the snowmelt, my frozen body was discovered.

In the fall, Hector Nice's final volume appeared from Verdoux Books.

NONE NUNS

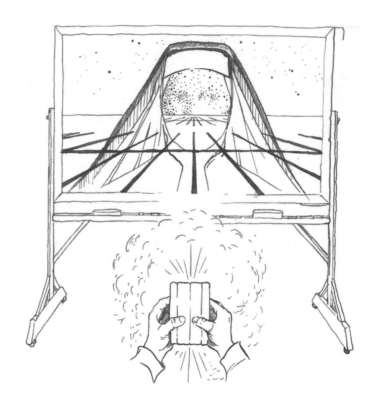

"Frankly, I was lucky to escape with just an eraser."

Meantime, for various reasons, he scarcely ever left the house.

George MacDonald, "The Cruel Painter" (1871)

There are none nuns in the parking lot, I wrote on the blackboard in chalk. I was seven; I knew better! It was obviously suspect. I knew you would say *no nuns,* not *none nuns.* But I'd been sent to the board to write a sentence with the word *none* in it, and I couldn't resist trying my hand at a little topical humor, nuns being highly topical to a bunch of seven-year-old schoolkids at St. Patrick's grammar school in Lawrence, MA. It was the wrong word but I tried to fit it in anyway. It'd be funny and I'd be hailed a hero by my peers.

BAP! My head rang, my eyes filled with tears, my lungs inhaled chalkdust. Sister Gregory had pegged me with an eraser, which was preferable to a piece of chalk or a rosary, both of which she wielded in her arsenal, but nonetheless still upsetting. I was called over to her desk to undergo the ritual humiliation of having my knuckles rapped with a ruler, then sent sniveling back to my seat while she angrily erased the blackboard. Some hero. At no point was the nature of my offense addressed, but she knew I knew why she'd clocked me one. As a rule, the Sisters of Charity of Halifax discouraged humor in the temple of learning, and they frequently mistook the most unintended irreverence for mockery. Frankly, I was lucky to escape with just an eraser.

What I have wondered since, however, is: why *parking lot?* It was fully incidental to the joke; I just needed a place where nuns would be none. Being an urban child, I would hardly have set them in a meadow, and the parking lot seemed like one of their natural habitats. I would see them in the church parking lot on Sundays and, during the week, our schoolyard essentially was a parking lot, just a small puddle of blacktop pooling to one side of the 19th-century brick school building, surrounded by a jail-like fence of iron spikes. (No dreaming spires, these!) And it was the '70s, there were lots of parking lots. I spent lots of time locked in cars waiting for a parent to finish doing something somewhere. Still, it seems a little random, a little odd, at this remove.

Forty years later, I find myself married and childless, living in San Francisco during a pandemic. I used to go to an office but now I work from home, so I seldom leave the house, and

my lifestyle is sedentary to an unhealthy degree. In an inef-
fectual effort to exercise, my wife and I have taken to an evening walk after I get off work, like 9 or 9:30, a couple of miles
in the hilly streets. It's not much but it's better than nothing.
We try to go every night, but we miss some nights.

Because we're in San Francisco, where the streetlight's
deliberately feeble to preserve the starlight, it is *dark*, midnight dark, at 9 at night in the winter. And it was on such a
dark winter's night, a Tuesday, that my wife and I donned our
masks and left our apartment in the Mission to stretch our
calves in Noe Valley. We head up 22nd to Church Street, and
walk down Church towards Day Street, between 29th and
30th. (Fun fact: I've only been on Day Street at night.) Just
before 29th, on the opposite side of the street, we approach
St. Paul's Catholic Church, the church, I assume, from
whence Church derives its name, and as we approach my
wife and I hear singing, not the cracked out caterwauling of
an urban evening but choral singing, ethereal, clearly em-
anating from a substantial body of women. It's not what you
expect in this neighborhood at night, certainly not on a week
night, amid the pandemic deserted streets. But there it was.

Just past the church is St. Paul's Elementary School, a
classic parish-style satellite, much like St. Patrick's, but even

closer, merely separated by a fenced-in a strip of asphalt that similarly doubles as schoolyard and parking lot. There are signs on the fence announcing sundry decrees and policies, and the fenceposts are much closer than the iron spikes of my alma mater, so it's hard to see into the yard from a distance, yet both my wife and I detect a veritable throng of nuns facing away from the street singing an adoration or supplication of or to some saint or god. We stop across the street just before the church and listen. But I'm not satisfied, my hearing is bad, and I say "Let's cross" as I plunge into the middle of the street. There's no traffic to worry about, though the few people in the immediate vicinity, like three or four, not counting pets, are similarly captivated, and have begun to accumulate on the sidewalk opposite.

But I have a plan. Being an old hand at nineteenth-century American Catholic church architecture, I've immediately sussed the building, and I bound up the front stairs, hidden by the concrete-covered granite slabs flanking the staircase, intending to peer over the topmost slab while remaining concealed from the inward-facing nuns. I reach the top and stealthily pop my head over the slab, to see what these nuns are up to.

As I do, I lock eyes with about 40 young nuns, who as it

turns out are not facing inward but rather to the side, singing to a statue of the Virgin Mary set into a niche just below where I'm standing. They are dressed in white saris and habits with the distinctive blue-striped border denoting Mother Teresa's Missionaries of Charity. For what seems like way too long a moment, I am frozen, transfixed by the gaze of these singing nuns, but I almost instantly duck back below the slab and am freed from the paralyzing spell of their eyes. My eyes begin to sweat, almost like they felt when old Sister Greg hit me in the head with an eraser.

It's all I can do to walk home with my wife in silence.

Throughout the pandemic, my wife and I have had a running argument about the purpose of our evening walks. To me, it's a discipline to keep us alive and I thrive on the unvaried routine of the measured two miles of exercise. To her it's an activity we do together and she'd like to vary the route so that we multiply our experiences together and enjoy our time outside at night after being cooped up all day in the apartment. But the next evening, there's no question of what we're going to do. We're going to walk up Church Street to St. Paul's, sight of our extraordinary encounter.

And as we approach the church from the opposite sidewalk, though we hear nothing, we both again see the throng of nuns from the previous night, as though they're milling about between numbers. We're a little later than the previous evening, and I remember hoping as we crossed the street that we hadn't missed the song. But when we arrive at the sidewalk in front of the church, to our astonishment, the schoolyard between the school and the church is utterly deserted. We were both so sure we'd seen them that we hadn't even needed to explain to each other. It was disquieting, to say the least.

Still, I couldn't resist trying to inject a little humor into the situation.

"There are none nuns in the parking lot!" I say.

Even in her disquiet, my wife turns to me and smiles. She knows the story. But as she does, I notice a small quantity of white particles accumulating on her shoulder. Chalkdust. I look up just in time to see the giant eraser falling from the sky.

THE SNEEZE

"The water in the mug continued to slowly circle
long after I'd ceased to stir it, then suddenly . . ."

I'd been at Naranjo 87 (87 Orange Tree Street) three or four weeks before I noticed it. At first all the noises were new, and Mexico City is noisy, but already the noises had begun to image the rounds of the neighborhood, and I heard the morning commute, schoolkids after school, nightlife, fucking, snoring, etc., which, if you're a layabout poet/translator type and spend the bulk of your time indoors pouring over ridiculous literature in multiple languages, helps keep you in touch with the rhythms of the day. Xochi contributed her share too, by needing to go for walks, trips to the vet, that sort of thing, and I'd connect the noises I'd been hearing to the places I was seeing on these excursions and build up my picture of the neighborhood. It had gone this way with every apartment I'd lived in in Mexico City.

So it was just at that point, when I'd woven a mental web sufficient to register and mostly ignore the noises of my surroundings so I could work on Marcel Schwob in peace, that I first noticed it. Every time I made a noise, like if I accidentally knocked a glass against a dish, or I answered the phone, or I addressed Xochi, or Xochi barked, or really just about anything, I would hear, as though muffled through the wall, a sneeze, one of genuine if exaggerated vigor, yet somehow also contemptuous, disapproving, a dismissive *blah, blah, blah* issued tit for tat with every incidental noise that manifested my presence to its unseen owner. I made some experiments to confirm the correlation but I quickly learned the sneeze refused to be drawn if it sensed you were deliberately trying to provoke it. And obviously sometimes the guy wasn't home, though these rare periods of tranquility seldom exceeded one or two hours. Whoever the sneeze was didn't work a 9 to 5. But just as I'd sink into true forgetfulness, unaware at last even of its absence, the sneeze would make its invasive return, as I wrestled, say, with a particularly knotty passage of "The Wooden Star."

I could block the sneeze out, of course, with music, though I preferred to write or translate in relative silence and often found all but the most ambient of soundtracks distracting. And sometimes I probably didn't notice, because the sound was muffled, after all, and whatever noise I was making, like grinding coffee, blocked it out. If anything, however, this simply made the sneeze more invasive, because, when I was feeling low, thinking perhaps of the relationship that drove me abroad in the first place, and in a moment of regret mingled with despair would heave a great involuntary sigh, the sneeze would follow militantly on its heels, mocking my sadness at the maximum point of fragility. When I myself sneezed, moreover, for a man must sneeze now and again, the sneeze would provide a faint, derisive echo of my own. This was somehow worse than its intrusions on my sorrow, and I found myself cursing it aloud, in English, and vowing to run it down to its source.

Which, of course, I eventually did. After a couple more days, I'd linked its reappearance following a noticed absence with the sound of keys in the corridor. The sneeze was clearly my next-door neighbor, with whom I shared the largest wall of my living room. We were the only two apartments on this end of the corridor. It had to be him. Still, I didn't immediately rush out on hearing his keys to identify my nemesis, but rather waited to cross paths with him naturally. Finally, one afternoon around 2:30, I was returning from the Alameda Central with Xochi as I saw the man turning the keys in the lock. I'd seen him before in the building, and even outside, a short, sinewy oldster, with gray, scarecrow-like hair that issued at wild angles from beneath the brim of a tattered straw hat, and a huge hooter of a nose that dominated his face. As I passed him in the corridor and nodded, he fixed on me what

I can only describe as a glare of absolute hatred. It was so disconcerting, I had to look away as I fumbled with Xochi's leash while patting my pockets to find my own keys. I heard the man slam the door, and then, as if to deliberately confirm his identity, there came the most ostentatiously contemptuous version of the sneeze that its author was capable of letting fly. It was the sneeze all right, and he didn't give a damn that I knew.

There followed, I confess, a period during which I attempted to woo him, lofting an overcheerful "Hola!" at every chance encounter on the street or in the building itself. Nothing. On the street, he would look straight through me, cutting me with all the dignity he could muster, while in the corridor his glare of hatred would deepen several shades. I couldn't understand why he had it out for me. Because I was a gringo? Surely I couldn't have been the worst he'd ever seen. I'd learnt Spanish, enough that I began translating it and was soon handling as much Spanish literature as French. Because I obviously didn't have a normal job, being home at all hours of the day? So was he! Though, of course, he was probably retired from some industrious profession he'd labored at for much of his life. Did he think I was rich? In Santa María la Ribera? I was here because I could live on almost nothing, and almost nothing was what I made from my various literary endeavors. Was that so wrong? I couldn't have this sort of life in the States, where I could drop everything and spend a week working on *Cartoons*, my own manuscript of writing inspired by the Latin American writers who'd been inspired by Marcel Schwob, whom I was introducing in translation to readers in the U.S., where he'd previously had no impact despite his outsized influence south of the Rio Grande. It was a complicated literary equation I was in the midst of. What business of his was it, how I spent my life? I'd never faced such a dilemma before, and I realized the past few years in Mexico City had gone remarkably easily, all things considered. Could I live with the sneeze? Should I admit defeat and move? But I'd just gotten the place and it'd been a tremendous pain in the ass to find a place that answered all my needs, which is why I'd already had so many apartments here. This place was almost perfect, save, of course, for the sneeze.

What brought the situation to its intolerable head was a cold. In the middle of summer, no less! I'd caught the worst cold I'd had in years, leaving me weak with exhaustion. I had to have Jero come over to walk Xochi, it was that bad. As I lay in bed, or on the couch, zoning out over Schwob's correspondence with Robert Louis Stevenson in a futile attempt to continue working, I'd be wracked with a convulsive series of sneezes, three or four in a row, which in my present state was enough to make me dizzy. The sneeze would patiently wait out the storm, then echo it through the wall in the exact same pattern, say, two in quick succession, with a third following after a two-beat pause. The sneeze was mocking me; it sounded cheerful, delighted with its mimicry while taking pleasure in my suffering. After a couple days of this, all I could think was, *you god damn mother fucker*, over and over as I lay back in near-delirium. Then the book would slide off my lap and hit the floor, and the sneeze would rub that in my face as well. I hated the sneeze, and I swore I would have my vengeance.

After a few days, I was well enough to emerge, in a fragile state, from the confines of the apartment and, at Jero's instruction, totter over to the Mercado de Sonora to buy dried gordolobo for a tea to combat the cold's lingering effects while he brought Xochi to Alameda Central to let her run off some of the week's pent up energy. Anything to get away from the sneeze, who seemed like he never went out anymore for sheer joy in my torment. I let the crowd carry me off the subway and down the concrete slope from the overpass toward the parking lot of the Mercado, which was itself much more a mercado in its own right than it was a parking lot, most of it being filled with mazelike rows of stalls and thus impossible to navigate by car. But I just drifted passively through the crowd until I was finally deposited inside the building, then, with slightly more deliberation and difficulty, made my way to the herb seller where I bought most of my herbs, by the cages of all-black roosters for sacrificial purposes. If that guy didn't have it, he would send me to someone who did, but he had a barrel of dried gordolobo right up front like he was waiting for me to arrive. He measured out a few grams and bagged them up for me.

Near the herb stall was a smaller stall whose main products were books on all manner of esoteric subjects and potions for various lifegoals involving love or finance, all jostling for the same shelf space. The potions were boxed like perfumes, with a cellophane window displaying the bottle, but they weren't facing out, so you could easily mistake the snazzily branded side of the box for the spine of a book and you never knew quite what you were laying hands on. The stall was just big enough for one customer to step one step inside to browse while the decidedly non-occult-looking owner sat at an improvised till half-inside/half-outside the stall, studying *Unomásuno*'s sports section. As I perused the titles, my hand came to rest on a black sleeve with gold embossed letters that said *El Estornudo*. Surely it couldn't be a potion, though *The Sneeze* was almost equally weird as the title of a book. Didn't Gogol have a story called *The Sneeze?* I wondered as I tugged at the top of the spine, only to encounter an unexpected resistance. I thought I must still be weak from the cold, but then I realized the spine was actually a lever, and as I pulled it down, a small area of the shelves turned inward, as though on a mechanism, revealing a dark corridor beyond. I looked at the owner, but his scrutiny of the sports section took on an added flare of intensity, as he determinedly ignored the opening of this portal. I glanced back out of the stall at my herb seller and he rolled his eyes towards the opening and raised his chin, as if to say, *go ahead, it's cool,* so without deliberating further, I plunged into the darkness of the corridor, only to hear the shelf snap closed behind me almost instantly.

It was too dark to see, but the corridor came to an end after only a few more steps. Almost instinctively, I reached for a doorknob and immediately felt one in my hand, which I turned. I entered a brightly lit room. It took my eyes a few seconds to adjust. The room was a clinically modern office interior, with an old woman in a white labcoat seated behind a desk, who motioned for me to sit at one of the two chairs in front of it. Behind the old woman's chair was a warren of various drawers and cubbyholes, with a sink and a cup dispenser next to it. I sat in the chair indicated, in stupefied silence, while the old woman regarded me kindly but seriously, like she was performing a silent intake exam. Her face was impossibly wrinkled, like she was of an extremely advanced age, yet her eyes and her movements seemed young, too graceful and carefree for an old woman.

After regarding me some minutes, she silently rose, went over to the warren, and opened a drawer, from which she withdrew a small envelope. She turned to the sink, pulled a cup from the dispenser, and poured the contents of the envelope into the cup. She filled the cup with water from the tap and then, oddly, I thought, given the medicinal air of the office, stuck her finger in the liquid and stirred it. Then she returned to the desk and handed me the cup. "Drink this, my child," she said, in Spanish, of course, and while I'm not generally in the habit of drinking finger-stirred drinks, I felt compelled to follow the old woman's commands. The liquid in the cup had taken on a faint yellow hue and, when drunk, had a mildly bitter, earthen taste to it. She took the empty cup from me, crushed it, and dropped it into a small, foot-operated trashcan beneath the sink. Then she reseated herself behind the desk, looked me over a few seconds, and smiled.

"That should take care of your cold," the old woman said. "Now tell me why you've come."

And, without giving it too much thought, except for how to phrase parts of it in Spanish, I poured out my tale of woe concerning the sneeze. She took in my words with a professional's good-natured gravity, occasionally raising an eyebrow at one detail or another, but only interrupting once to ask, "Schwob? An influence on Bolaño, no?" "Yes," I said, "and Borges," and was about to launch into a discussion of how Borges claimed *A Universal History of Infamy* was inspired by *Imaginary Lives*, thus putting Schwob at the very origins of magic realism so-called, but she waved this topic away before I could begin and I resumed my grievances against the sneeze.

After I was finished, she sat silently behind the desk, musing with her eyes half-closed and her palms together, tapping her fingertips against her lips for several moments. Then she stood and turned back to the warren, standing on a small step stool so she could reach the top row of drawers. She opened one, pulled an object out of it, then closed it, stepped down, and stooped to open another drawer near the bottom of the warren. She withdrew a small envelope much like the first one, closed the drawer, then seated herself back at her desk. She dropped the envelope and the object onto her desk blotter. The object looked like a piece of dried seaweed. She opened a drawer in her desk, pulled out a small pad of stationary, and reached for one of the two elegant pens which stood in a penholder at the edge of her desk. She scribbled on the pad for a minute or so, then tore off the sheet, and folded it in half. Then she wheeled her chair back to open the slim tray under the desktop, from which she produced a sheet of butcher paper, a ball of twine, and a tiny golden pair of scissors. She wrapped the envelope, the piece of seaweed, and the instructions in the paper, which she tied into a neat parcel with a length of twine snipped with her golden scissors. She handed the parcel over to me.

"Follow these instructions carefully, and the sneeze will trouble you no more," she said, smiling reassuringly.

"How much do I . . . ?" I began, patting my pockets. She smiled again and shook her head. Then she gestured toward the door.

"I'm afraid I have another consultation," she said.

I took the hint, stood from my chair, and headed to the door. As I opened the door, a man wearing an enormous ruff and a great plumed hat strode in. His brow furrowed in displeasure, as though we were passing each other in the waiting room of a clinic for a highly specific and humiliating ailment. I quickly slid past him and closed the door behind me.

When I came to, I found myself stretched out on my couch in my apartment. Had it been a dream? No, the parcel was there on the coffee table next to me, as was the bag of gordolobo. As a writer, I had to admire it, for if you have a magic corridor at your disposal and you don't use it to immediately shift the setting to where the next scene takes place, you're a fool. I sat up and stretched. There was a note from Jero saying I'd been so out of it by the time I got back to the apartment, he'd taken Xochi back to his place so I could sleep off the cold without interruption. He also left instructions for making an infusion of gordolobo. But as the old woman had promised, my cold was gone. I felt refreshed even. I stretched again, and yawned. Immediately, the sneeze was on me, like it'd been waiting out my extended slumber just to launch one. My eye fell on the parcel. A chorus of *you god damn mother fucker*s swelled within my breast. The twine untied at the lightest tug. I unfolded the instructions and got to work.

In the kitchen, I filled the kettle as instructed. The sneeze protested here and there, but it was always a bit baffled by a running spigot and only sprang back to life when I put the kettle on the stove. I lit the burner with the loudest wooden match I had on hand, and the sneeze sneezed, but with less conviction, like it knew I was up to something and was nervous. As I waited for the water to boil, I looked through the cabinet to find a suitable mug, making as much crockery on crockery noise as I could. The sneeze fell silent. I found a Sanborns promotional mug of sufficient volume for the deed. I placed the piece of dried seaweed from the parcel into the mug and tore open the envelope and emptied it in as well. It contained less than a teaspoon of large, loose granules, about the consistency of ground coffee, but off-white instead of black. The kettle whistled, prompting a single sullen sneeze from the sneeze. I turned off the burner, grabbed the kettle and hooked the handle of the mug on the index finger of the same hand, leaving me a hand for keys and doorknobs. At the door, I slipped into some slippers, stepped into the corridor, and locked the door behind me, hearing as I did one final faint sneeze of protest as I turned the key.

The basement of our building was not for the faint of heart. It was damp and moldy, with corpses of rats half-eaten by other rats laying in traps seemingly scattered at random. Bugs crawled along the walls with careless abandon, like you were in their domain. Other unseen creatures made their presence known through various scurryings and squealings. There was a faint light given off by an equivocal bulb, which flickered from time to time like it was on the verge of going out altogether. But there were pipes running overhead, with the occasional unit number spray-painted thereon to guide any plumber brave enough to service such an establishment and I followed these numbers until I was directly below the sneeze's apartment.

I poured hot water from the kettle into the mug and then set the kettle on the floor. I was supposed to stir the seaweed and the granules but I'd forgotten to bring a spoon, so with some reluctance dipped my finger into the mug. To my astonishment, the fluid had already grown cold and viscous, nauseatingly so, and I stirred the concoction as best I could, drying my finger on my pantleg. The instructions had ended there, so I wasn't sure what would happen next. The water in the mug continued to slowly circle long after I'd ceased to stir it, then suddenly there arose from the mug the head and half the body of a huge, gray snake. The hideous creature stretched up its head towards the ceiling of the basement, then began to move its head backwards and forwards, with a slow oscillating motion, as if looking for something. At last the snake made a sudden dart, and clung to the ceiling with its mouth. I slowly lowered the mug until the snake was fully clear of it, then picked up the kettle and made my way back upstairs as fast as I possibly could.

I'd be lying if I said I didn't find the experience of conjuring up such an unexpected demon disconcerting. Yet I was pleasantly surprised to find that the procedure had worked as advertised. For the rest of day, even when Jero came back with Xochi, the sneeze was silenced. I fancied I heard, once or twice, *something*, as though the sneeze were attempting to sneeze, but couldn't, but this might have been my imagination and in any case was so faint as to be almost undetectable. Whatever that magic seaweed snake was doing worked.

There followed two of the pleasantest days I had known since moving to Mexico City. It was precisely because they were so ordinary that I enjoyed them. I played with Xochi, took her on walks, translated Schwob, made any number of inadvertent noises, and—nothing! No sneeze took it upon itself to criticize my actions and lifestyle, to mock my moments of despair or joy. It was blissful, and I peeled off page after page of Schwob in English, plus a couple of poems of my own. I felt a buoyancy I hadn't felt in some time, if ever.

The next day I left my apartment around noon to take

Xochi for a walk in the park. I'd had such a productive couple days, I felt carefree, and was thinking about heading to Jero's afterward to drink old-fashioneds. As I headed down the street, I saw the old man from next door on his way home. He looked exhausted, almost withered, as he trudged up the sidewalk, though when he saw me, he drew himself to his full height to cut me as I passed. I turned around only to see his shoulders immediately sink in fatigue, like the effort of drawing himself up had cost him a greater share of his vitality than he could afford. I felt triumphant, though I had to admit I also felt an unanticipated twinge of guilt. But what could I do? I had to stop the sneeze, but I had no way of calibrating the effect on the man himself. Still, the guilt lingered. The next time I saw him, a few days later, he'd withered away to an even greater extent, merely throwing me a dull look of hatred as I passed him in the corridor. Soon even this became too much for him and he couldn't bother to look at me, so consumed was he by his own physical suffering. He'd grown notably gaunt and frail, and it'd only been a little over a week since he'd lost his sneeze. Surely I couldn't be causing all this!

The next afternoon, as I was returning from a walk with Xochi, I came across the old man being helped up the stairs by a young woman, around my age. She was a dark-haired beauty, with just the barest hint of the same oversized nose that manifested itself on her dad's mug to such spectacular effect. I imagined *her* sneezing and how different it would feel, coming from her. She was carrying plastic bags from the pharmacy and the old man leant on her for support. I held the door for the pair as they struggled inside. He didn't seem to recognize me. As they passed, I even heard a throttled *gracias* rasp out of his parched throat.

After that he stopped going out. But I continued to see the young woman come and go, bringing groceries and more supplies from the pharmacy. We would smile at one another when we met and her smile was warm and genuine but also conveyed an unbearable depth of sadness. Once I came home from an errand just as she was wrestling an old aluminum walker up the front stairs, and I insisted on carrying it for her. She thanked me at her door. "My father is not well," she said, almost apologetically, as if to explain her continued presence. I nodded, but couldn't speak, knowing, however much I tried to rationalize it away, I was the author of her profound distress. I no longer felt triumphant.

The next time I saw her, I nearly bumped into her as Xochi and I were leaving the apartment. She was startled, but to my astonishment she fell into my arms and began to sob violently. I can't lie; the feeling of her body against mine was electric, despite every feeling of dispassionate human concern I could muster. It was over in seconds and she willed herself into composure almost instantly, dabbing at her eyes with a handkerchief. She smiled painfully.

"My father is dying," she said.

I nodded.

"I'm sorry," I said.

"Do you mind if I smoke?" she asked.

"Please!"

She was waiting outside while a doctor examined her father, she explained, offering me a cigarette. I turned it down, but I stayed with her while she smoked in silence. But she only got in a few drags before the door to the old man's apartment opened and the doctor motioned her inside. She smiled at me apologetically and went back inside without another word. I stood in the corridor a few moments, Xochi looking at me anxiously, then returned to my apartment, and the dog followed, murmuring disapproval. I had to do something.

I'm not in the business of uninstalling magic seaweed snakes, so my supply of appropriate tools was limited. After rummaging around for a while, with Xochi following me closely from room to room, I managed to accumulate a hammer, a dull steak knife, and a pair of salad tongs. It was not an arsenal that inspired confidence and, supposing I did actually dislodge the beast from the basement ceiling, I didn't even have a container to put it in. I thought of the Sanborns mug, but clearly that was no use at this point. After considering a stock pot and a shopping bag, I eventually settled on a pillowcase. Surely I wouldn't emerge from this contest alive, but I thought again of the old man's daughter, and I knew I had to try. I put my tools in the pillowcase and slung it over my shoulder.

Xochi sensed something was afoot and stayed at my heels as I slipped into the corridor and locked my door. I was touched by her loyalty and concern. I'd found her on the street a couple years ago, so hopefully, if I didn't make it, she'd be able to survive until someone else took pity on her. Together, we crept down to the basement. The old lightbulb seemed even dimmer than last time. I tried to approach with stealth, as if that would help, following the spray-painted numbers with increasing dread. Suddenly we were upon it; the gray snake remained in the same position, fangs sunk into the ceiling, but it seemed heavy and swollen, stretching nearly to the floor. It took no notice of us. I unslung the pillowcase from my shoulder and looked inside, trying to determine which instrument was most likely to dislodge the demon from the ceiling. Had I really brought salad tongs? Suddenly, Xochi began to growl, the hair rising on her back, and before I could even turn to shush her, she sprang into action. The whole scene seemed to take place in slow motion as I watched her fly through the air, jaws open wide, and then sink her teeth into the snake's gray flesh. I heard a huge bang and felt myself thrown violently to the ground. I found myself laying in a viscous pool of clear liquid. Xochi was immediately by my side, bewildered, covered in the same disgusting fluid as I was, but seemingly unharmed. She opened her mouth wide and then yacked up a piece of dried seaweed, as though the gray snake had reverted to its original form. I felt sore all over. As I lay there attempting to gather my wits, I heard an extremely faint rhythmic sound, like a handsaw, coming from above. *AH−, AH−, AH−, AH−, AH−, AH−*

Despite the pain, I leapt to my feet.

"Run, Xochi!" I hollered as we sped back to the stairs, which already seemed to be warping and twisting under my feet as I climbed.

It was going to blow.

THE LEMON

"The black-haired hand held itself out,
wordlessly demanding the lemon."

Among the few perks working the overnight shift at the front desk of the Hyatt in Hampton, VA, believe it or not, are the celebrity sightings. The hotel's an inch away from the Coliseum, and there are no deluxe hotels in Hampton to accommodate a sizeable crew, so the Hyatt punches above its weight. You might see a big movie star comedian like Kevin Hart, or a Christian megabastard like Joel Osteen, but mostly it's musicians. Anyone from a young douche like Justin Bieber to a grizzled roadster like George Thorogood to a living legend like Bob Dylan. You might get P-Funk *and* Earth Wind & Fire on the same package tour, or see a beefy bodyguard tote Ariana Grande around like an exotic python. Make a new keycard for Eric Church or guide an inebriated Ying Yang Twin back to his room. It's not every night; some evenings at the Coliseum are devoted to more anonymous spectacles like bullriding or monster trucks or Disney on Ice. But musicians of varying levels of fame are frequent enough to keep you on your toes.

You gotta be cool and professional, and you get blasé after

a while. And you age out of it; I once mistook BTS for a group of South Korean entrepreneurs staying on a different floor. I figured they were in cosmetics or skincare. So I barely raised an eyebrow when, as I clocked in and Ol' Marilyn clocked out, she told me in hushed tones that Ringo Starr & His All-Starr Band were in the building. Now if this had been 1989, say, when Joe Walsh, Dr. John, Billy Preston, and about half the Band were in the group, I might've been impressed. But the wattage of the All-Starr Band had since dimmed considerably. Colin Hay (Men at Work) and Gregg Rolie (Santana, Journey) splitting a bucket of beers and some garlic fries wasn't exactly gossip column fare; even TMZ would tell you to fuck off.

So I forgot all about it; I had Bolaño's *Savage Detectives* with me and got down to it, with only the most fleeting interruptions. When, in the middle of the crazy blow job scene in the first part of the novel, the front desk phone rang around 3 a.m., I barely paused reading long enough to give a "Front desk, how can I help you?"

The voice on the other end was British—regional, working-class British—and oddly familiar, though I didn't place it.

"I asked for a lemon."

"Pardon me?"

"I asked for a lemon; I was told there'd be a lemon for me in the suite."

"Oh, I'm terribly sorry, Mister ...," I pecked the suite number on the keyboard, looked at the screen, and suddenly swallowed hard. ".... Starkey." Holy shit—Ringo! I checked the activity log. "It says here we left you some lemons, but we must have made a mistake."

"They're slices."

"I beg your pardon?"

"Lemon slices. I need a whole lemon, a lemon I can squeeze."

"Of course!" I said, not knowing what I meant. "We'll send up a lemon at once; is there anything else?"

"Just the lemon," he said, tersely, hanging up. I slowly placed the receiver on the hook and stood frozen at the desk, pondering the magnitude. I'd just spoken with a Beatle! Granted it was only Ringo, one-time pitchman for Sun Country Wine Coolers during a particularly low ebb in the '80s, but now Sir Richard, knight of Her Majesty's realm. Fully half the surviving band. Technically, in the artistic scheme of things, I should have been more excited about Nobel Laureate Dylan, but all I ever got out of Dylan was, "Is there any more of that hazelnut creamer?" Ringo and I had *conversed*. About a lemon. Ringo needed a lemon. At 3 a.m. The booking terminal said 3:03, and this was enough to snap me out of my stupor and launch me into action.

The kitchen was under lock and key at this hour, but all I needed to do was slip into the men's room from the lobby, hit the inner door with my keycard, and bam, I was in Mingles, the hotel bar. And I wasn't alone. J. D. the bartender was still behind the bar, cleaning idly, but actually drinking margies with Ol' Marilyn and some schlubby fella I'd never seen, clearly a guest, not a coworker.

"Hey, chief!" J. D. called everyone "chief" to save him the trouble of remembering names, so I was surprised at first when he then addressed me by name. "Hey, Claude. This is Steve Lukather. You know, the guy from Toto!"

I knew nothing of the sort. But I accepted his proffered mitt.

"Nice to meet you," Steve Lukather said.

"Meet you all the way," I said.

Steve Lukather rolled his eyes. I didn't have time for this.

"Listen, J. D., you got a lemon?"

"Right here, chief," he said, indicating a plastic tub of lemon wedges, next to the olives and cherries.

"No, I need a whole lemon," I said. "Uncut."

"This a grocery store, chief?" J. D. said, instantly territorial over what was in fact the Hyatt's lemon supply. I didn't have time for this either. I was about to pull rank, but was saved from this unseemly display by Steve Lukather.

"I bet it's for Ringo," he said. "Ringo and his lemons!" J. D. shot me a look like, "Seriously?" and I nodded with all the solemnity I could muster against the pastel backdrop of Mingles' ocean-themed interior.

"No kidding?" Ol' Marilyn said, while J. D. bent to rummage around the below-bar fridge. "What's he need lemons for?"

"His voice," Steve Lukather said. "He's got a special formula he gargles with; it's like brandy, honey, lemon juice, vinegar, some other stuff. Same recipe George Harrison used on the *Dark Horse* tour."

"Jeez, that must work," I said, alluding to George's notorious laryngitis during that star-crossed outing. Steve Lukather glared at me like I'd told him to fuck the rain down in Africa. Fortunately, J. D. popped up from behind the bar with a lemon.

"OK, chief," he said, "I was gonna make twists with this, but this one's for Ringo; tell him J. D. sent it."

"Sure."

As I headed to the men's room to return to the lobby, he called after me.

"That's a lemon you owe me."

Back in the lobby, the clock read 3:08. I was wasting precious minutes. At this hour, I might have run up to the deluxe suites without worrying about coverage, but what if Ringo invited me in and regaled me with stories about filming *Caveman* (1981)? Unlikely, but I needed to be ready. We were only 500 miles from Nashville; what if he wanted to reminisce about recording his country album *Beaucoups of Blues* (1970)? I had to allow, in other words, for the possibility of a personal encounter with the conductor emeritus of *Shining Time Station*.

I paged Raoul, the night porter, from the front desk. It was never clear where Raoul absconded to when he wasn't actively assisting guests, but as long as he turned up when paged, I couldn't worry about it. In this case, he came in from outside through the automatic doors, in a cloud of cigarette smoke.

"Yes, boss?"

"I need you to watch the desk for a minute," I said, brandishing the lemon, "while I bring this upstairs."

Raoul held out his hand.

"Want me to take it?"

"No," I said, instinctively concealing it in the pocket of my Hyatt-issued blazer. "V.I.P. service. Just watch the desk a minute and I'll be right back." Raoul shrugged.

"Yes, boss." He went behind the desk and immediately began leafing through *The Savage Detectives* without so much as a by-your-leave. But I didn't have time for it. I headed to the elevator bank and soon was on the fifth floor, where the deluxe suites are. Despite its size, this Hyatt's more horizontal than vertical, so fifth's the best we can do. Ringo was in suite 500, all the way down the hall to the left. I checked the time. 3:11. Not bad, all things considered.

Yet I hesitated. My left hand gripped the lemon tightly while my right hung frozen in air, failing to knock. I felt unexpected terror. I tried to compose myself. Phlegm gathered in my throat and I involuntarily cleared it, which seemed to make a deafening sound in the otherwise noiseless corridor and ultimately forced my hand.

"Room service," I said, with a discreet two-knock knock.

An eternity of silence seemed to elapse. I hesitated to knock again, given the lateness of the hour and my terror of the man I was trying to summon. I listened hard. I thought I might have heard some adenoidal noises from deep within the suite. Then I definitely heard the creak of a door, a faint jingle as of keys or belt buckle, and I prayed to that god I don't believe in except in moments of fear that I hadn't just interrupted the drummer of the Beatles during a shit. I heard some carpet-cushioned footsteps approach the door, saw the peephole briefly darken, and heard the sound of a series of latches unlatching and bolts unbolting. I steeled myself for a face-to-face encounter with the one and only Billy Shears. The knob turned and the door slowly began to open.

Kkkkkthung!

The door had only opened about four inches, abruptly halted by the taut length of chain. Through the opening a hand appeared, a hoary old brace of fingers with large knuckles, attached to a surprisingly hirsute wrist. Below one of the knuckles was a large silver ring, with a jeweled inlay in the shape of a star. The black-haired hand held itself out, wordlessly demanding the lemon. I slowly placed it in this imperious palm, and the once-blistered fingers of "Helter Skelter" fame closed around it like a tarantula seizing its prey. The hand began to pull, and in an instant I realized I couldn't let go of the lemon.

A fury boiled up within me. Was Ringo giving me the high hat? Not even facing me, or thanking me, after I'd tracked

down a squeezable lemon at this ungodly hour! Who'd he
think I was, Raoul? The hand, meanwhile, unaccustomed to
its desires being thwarted, was furious, pulling with all its
might. Was he not going to say anything? No "Let go of the
lemon, you twat"? No anecdotes from *Beaucoups of Blues*?
"Goddamn it, Ringo!" I heard myself say. "It don't come
that easy!"

I grabbed his hand with both of mine and began to pull,
but instead of resisting, the arm immediately gave, stretching
like a hairy, pale-skinned strip of taffy. And as I kept pulling
I soon had to let go of the hand itself in order to keep pulling this strip, though as I pulled the tenor of its resistance
changed and I felt more like I was unspooling some huge reel
of cord or cable or even chain. And as this reel unspooled it
took on the aspect of certain incidents in the life of Ringo
Starr. It's hard to describe, but it was sort of like that massive
Diego Rivera mural, *Pan American Unity* (1940), if each
panel depicted some representative scene focused on the
Beatle drummer, but there was still a linear aspect to the unspooling as the images went by. At times it felt like it was a
montage set to "Ringo's Theme," the instrumental version of
"This Boy" from the *Hard Day's Night* (1965) soundtrack, but
the imagery clashed with it, like harshly lit videotape from

his ill-fated variety show special *Ringo* (1978), but then it seemed to open up like a sublime vista of clouds set to the opening drums of "Back Off, Boogaloo," but mixed uneasily against the orchestral passage of "A Day in the Life," and it looked more like Ringo's pre-Beatle nightclub days with Rory Storm and the Hurricanes, in a bright red suit, beard, and pompadour, yet it was still somehow his unspooling arm and it seemed to be accumulating in massive tangled coils behind me filling up the corridor leading back to the elevators, and I thought surely I'd gone well past the arm by now and was drawing on some more essential core of Ringo, getting deep in the weeds of *Beaucoups of Blues*, which is far and away his best solo album for its unity of vision and how utterly suited the project is to his limited but very real charms as a vocalist, and constitutes the closest thing to a Beatles/Elvis collab, since D. J. Fontana plays some of the drums, the Jordanaires sing backing vocals, and even Scotty Moore is there for some strange reason engineering the sessions, and then it ended abruptly like I'd pulled the whole thing off the roll and I was left holding Ringo's other hand. And throughout the entire unspooling my ears were ringing with a steady tintinnabulation of Beatlemania teen girl shrieking and my nostrils stung by the acrid scent of orgasmic urinary release said to accompany those public outbursts of collective hysteria, until I realized I was the one screaming and copiously pissing my pants in front of a concerned Gregg Rolie, who was standing in the doorway of a nearby suite in his complimentary Hyatt bathrobe.

I stopped screaming and I heard the elevator ding and open, and out popped Steve Lukather and Ol' Marilyn, drunkenly giggling, but they pulled up short when they registered the scene they'd just stumbled into. Ol' Marilyn's eyes went wide.

"Again?!?!" Steve Lukather said.

He immediately began rummaging through the coils of Ringo and found the hand clutching the lemon, which he pried from the fingers. He started peeling the lemon, glaring at me, then dismissed the thought and turned to Ol' Marilyn instead.

"We're gonna need more lemons."

VYVYAN SOURMAN

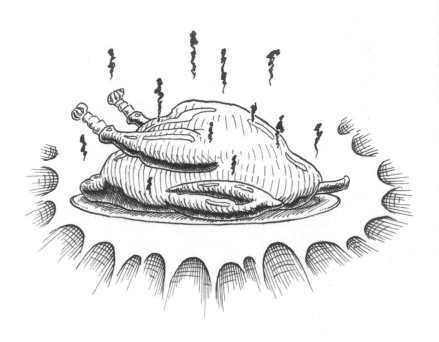

". . . a giant roast turkey complete with all the trimmings . . ."

It had been an uncharacteristically quiet winter afternoon at Verdoux Books, in the North Beach neighborhood of San Francisco, California. My boss was out having lunch with Patti Smith, there were no events scheduled in the store, and even the shaggy accordionist who routinely tortured us from across the street with his four-song repertoire—the unquestionable highlight of which was the *Star Wars* theme—had taken a rare sabbatical. I'd knocked back a couple weed gummies so I could force myself to write a letter to Éditions Fragonard, trying to persuade the bastards to let us print a translation of André Trombone's *Troubadour Périscopique* without demanding some absurd fee for the rights. You try being an American editor persuading a French publisher you have no money. *C'est incroyable!*

The gummies were just starting to hit when Irma ran in. We shared a thin sliver of office between the boss's office and marketing/publicity.

"Claude!"

"What?"

"You'd better come outside," she said. "Your name is in the sky."

I followed Irma downstairs and out the in door to the corner of Columbus and Broadway; she pointed toward the Bay, and sure enough, "TO CLAUDE GRIND" was floating in giant white letters against an otherwise clear blue sky. Even as we gaped in astonishment, an ampersand emerged below the "T" of "TO." By the time the skywriter had reached the "E" of what would likely be "VERDOUX BOOKS," I knew what was going on, and I couldn't stop myself from shaking my fist and bellowing:

"VYVYAN!!!!"

much to the astonishment of a pair of German tourists exiting the store. I realized I was really stoned. But there was no time to lose. Irma and I ran back inside and upstairs to the office. As I hurriedly packed my Verdoux Books shoulder bag, including my gummies and my bottle of Dr. Johnson's Fortifying Tonic for Editors, she printed out a contract and handed it to me. She wasn't even attached to the project, but I'd been droning on about it for years, so she needed no explanation. Still, her eyes widened when I pulled out the hunting knife I'd bought up the street at Columbus Cutlery and began strapping the scabbard to my thigh.

"Do you think that's necessary?" she asked.

"I hope not," I said. "But I'm not taking any chances."

I ran downstairs and out the in door again, then remembered how old I was as I wheezed up Columbus toward Vallejo St., where my car was parked. The huge knife strapped to my thigh considerably impeded my progress, and I eventually had to take it off and chuck it in my bag. Meanwhile, the skywriter, or rather I should say, Vyvyan Sourman—for it was he, son of the late French poet Cleo Sourman, a translation of whom we were publishing in the spring—was overhead rendering with some precision paragraph 3b of a standard Verdoux Books contract, even as most of the previously rendered clauses had already drifted away into the ether.

Minutes later I was tearing through the Broadway Tunnel toward Van Ness. But it was already 4:30, and traffic on the other side was snarled by shitheads making illegal lefts. And the lefts were all the slower as the shitheads caught sight of the skywriting behind me and dawdled mid-turn to decipher contractual information concerning musical performance rights. "Goddamn it, Vyvyan," I fumed, leaning on my horn in impotent rage. Why couldn't he just sign the contract, like a normal person? Then again, nothing in my dealings with Vyvyan Sourman had indicated he even remotely resembled a normal person.

Look, I have a Ph.D. in literature; I get it. Artists live unconventional lives and make unconventional parents. Their offspring are bound to be peculiar. Generally, these fall into two camps: those that hate the parent and those that worship the parent. Either variety may be crushed under the metaphysical weight of the parent's glory and either is capable of inhibiting the parent's reputation for spite or cynically exploiting it for profit. There are only about four or five variables to the calculus, though very occasionally I run across a guy like Anselm Berrigan, who seems so much better adjusted an adult than I that it gives the lie to my whole system. Still, like many systems, mine works to a point, enough to handle the vast majority of literary progeny I encounter.

But unlike Anselm, whose contradiction of the system simply confirmed its general applicability, Vyvyan Sourman seemed to confound it altogether. He had the unruffled surface opacity of the old-world aristocrat, having been born into the fabulous wealth of his exiled-by-revolution parents. Yet he managed to convey a scrupulous regard for his mother's work and posthumous reputation, even as he displayed the weary indolence of the most pampered scion, a near-paralysis that routinely threatened to derail the varied projects to which he'd nominally lent his approval. He seldom, for example, condescended to communicate directly with a publisher, usually hiding behind proxies like translators and scholars, and his standing policy was that he would sign a contract but he would not discuss anything. He was clearly unmotivated by money—in fact, was quite generous with his various collaborators—and he didn't display a trace of the filial rancor of notorious offspring like Paul Zukofsky, who seemingly sought to consign his father's work to oblivion. Vyvyan Sourman, in short, was inscrutable.

After much pleading, cursing, and laying on the horn, I'd finally inched my way up Broadway to Laguna, where I took a right, glancing up as I did so to see what paragraph Vyvyan was on: 12e. There wasn't much time. I was headed to the old abandoned airstrip on Laguna by Moscone Park. It was only a hunch, but I assumed a character like Vyvyan wouldn't launch such a sortie from SFO or Oakland International. The vine-strewn decay of the defunct Laguna Regional was much more in keeping with his style, and convenient to the tennis courts. It'd be like him to get in a few sets before or after his airborne shenanigans. Not that I'd spent any time with him, of course, and indeed had only elicited the curtest of responses to email queries futilely designed to not annoy him. For you don't have to be in the trade to know that publishing a deceased poet's work without at least minimal consultation with the rightsholder is damn-near impossible. Rights are complicated; the laws of the European Union and the United States differ considerably; and Cleo Sourman is a historically important poet. Even if, as a woman and a foreigner, she's shamefully neglected in France, she's not entirely out of print, so you need to verify whether any particular work is encumbered. And the French publisher is no help; you could ask a French publisher if they had rights to the alphabet and they'd say *yes*, just in case there was money at stake.

Having tangled with French publishers myself, I had no small understanding of Vyvyan's antipathy, even if it unfairly extended to those of us seeking to advance the reputation of his mother abroad. But still, this is business; if I make a wrong move, Verdoux could get sued, or have to pulp a book, neither of which would augur well for my position. It was my job to make sure such things didn't happen. One frank conversation with Vyvyan would have cleared up 99% of my concerns, but he had been adamant in his stance not to have this conversation. I even wrote him when I was in Paris the previous year, offering to take him to lunch any day of the week, just so I could ask the five or so questions I needed answers to. He claimed to be out of town on business! What business? I doubted he'd ever held a job in his life. I scoured the internet for intelligence, but he'd been remarkably circumspect in his dealings with the world. I could find but one photograph of the man, shaking hands with the honorary chairman of some charity gala he'd attended, even as his eye furtively avoided the camera. But it was clearly the Vyvyan Sourman I was after. I could see his mother's face peering from behind his features, despite the distance of gender and era. And really, how many Vyvyan Sourmans could there be?

Occasionally, in publishing, you're driven to take actions you're not proud of, and this was one of those times. I managed to wiggle Vyvyan's street address out of the translator I'd been dealing with on the pretext of sending a contract. Like everything about Vyvyan, even the address seemed unreal, an apartment building in the 16th arrondissement hard against the Bois de Boulogne. Who lives *there*? I arrived in the neighborhood early one morning, determined to surprise Vyvyan in the wild and ask the questions I needed to ask before we could proceed with publishing his mother's work. It was a grotesque violation of privacy, though no more grotesque than the lie this gadabout was attending to imaginary out-of-town business, and I was too close to my quarry to abandon pursuit. I lingered across the street, imperfectly concealed behind some trees, and waited. I pretended to be birding, with a well-thumbed copy of *Guide des oiseaux de Paris* in my back pocket and a discreet pair of field glasses that I trained on the building and the various personages who came and went.

Would I even recognize him? I didn't know. Yet when, after I'd waited several fruitless hours, a man emerged shrouded in a dark overcoat, a huge slouch hat, and a long red scarf, and began rapidly walking toward the Avenue Henri Martin, I knew it had to be Vyvyan and took off in pursuit, careful to keep a reasonable distance without losing him. He never looked behind him, or anywhere besides the pavement in front of him, like a man who knows he's being followed but hopes to conceal this knowledge, betraying himself through the exaggerated determination not to look back. But how, I wondered, could he suspect my presence? I'd acted like I'd believed him; perhaps it was too obviously an act. Perhaps he'd spied me from a window, with some binoculars of his own. However I'd revealed my hand, I grew certain from his brisk pace and his aforementioned determination: the game was afoot.

After about 15 minutes, he suddenly scurried into the Metro at the Rue de la Pompe, and I figured I had him trapped. I already had a day pass, so I followed him past the ticket window, through the turnstile, and over to the inbound platform, where a train was just pulling up. As I saw him enter a car, I boarded at the opposite end, determined to collar him before the next station. Through the crowd, I could see his hat and scarf, and as the train began to move, I relaxed, knowing he couldn't possibly escape. Yet, as I squeezed past various passengers, mostly pensioners and mothers with strollers at this time of day, I glanced out the window, only to see Vyvyan Sourman standing calmly on the platform, fanning himself with his hat and mopping his brow with a snow-white handkerchief. Our eyes met for the briefest instant before I was whisked into the darkness of the tunnel.

I was too surprised to be pissed; how had he escaped the train once it started moving? I sat down in confusion, impeded by the *Guide des oiseaux*, which I pulled from my pocket and threw on the floor. An old Frenchman in a beret shot me a dirty look, so I sheepishly picked up the book. He nodded with evident satisfaction. As we pulled into Trocadéro, I watched as he rose from his seat, approached the door, and, as the train was slowing to a stop but still moving, opened the latch. Of course! I'd forgotten the doors on the older Metro cars were self-service, a responsibility American straphangers quite obviously couldn't be trusted with. Vyvyan had simply let himself out before the doors automatically locked between stations. I had to hand it to the old villain, it was well played. I would have resumed my stakeout of his building, but I had to give a poetry reading that night at the old Théâtre Molière, so I returned to my hotel in defeat. And I was simply too busy for the rest of my trip. Vyvyan had bested me, at least that round.

Still, I'm not entirely without resources or I wouldn't have lasted this long in publishing. Once back in Frisco, using a combination of French friends, luck, and my own time-consuming researches, I determined to my reasonable satisfaction that Vyvyan's claim to the foreign rights of his mother's work was for the most part unimpaired, save for a handful of titles easy enough to leave aside. Cleo Sourman had plenty to choose from. The moment, therefore, had theoretically come; I told my boss she could schedule our translation for the upcoming season and give me a contract for Vyvyan to sign. Normally at this distance, I'd send a PDF to the rightsholder, who would print, sign, and scan it, but you'd sooner ask a Parisian to move the Eiffel Tower a few inches left than to scan something. *Printing* a PDF in Paris could bring down the government, let alone scanning one. Yet to my surprise, when I asked Vyvyan if he wanted me to mail him two copies of the contract to sign and return by post or whether I should email a PDF, he chose the latter. Perhaps, I reasoned, as a man of means, he could accomplish this normally prohibitive feat, or maybe Paris kept its scanner in the Bois de Boulogne. It'd save postage, at any rate, so I happily attached the PDF to my reply. I figured he'd dick around with it for a few days, and who knows how many days it takes to get something scanned in Paris, so let's say, two weeks I'd give him before I'd send a follow up query.

Much to my surprise, I received an email within the week, with a JPEG worrisomely attached. I should have known it was too good be true. I clicked on the file and opened it up in Preview. It was a photograph of two hands holding a somewhat rumpled sheet of paper, on which was printed a shrunken version of the two-page Editions Verdoux contract, signed at the bottom "Vyvyan Sourman." On closer inspection, the contract wasn't even complete; clauses had been jammed together willy nilly, piling up on one another in a jumble of incoherence, in order to fit on one sheet. It was madness. It certainly wouldn't do as a legal document, and how was my boss supposed to countersign a JPEG? Goddamn it, Vyvyan.

I glanced around the office. Irma was absorbed in a spreadsheet calculating royalties. In my right ear, I could hear my boss chatting on speakerphone with Tom Waits and in my left I could hear a meeting underway in marketing/publicity. I reached into my bag, found my bottle of Dr. Johnson's Fortifying Tonic for Editors, and took a quick but satisfying pull. I took a couple gummies, took a deep breath, took stock on the question of whether or not I still wanted to spend my life dealing with maniacs like this, and then calmly wrote to Vyvyan to explain with as much cordiality as I could muster that a JPEG of a signed contract wouldn't serve our purposes, and I reiterated my offer to send a pair of printed contracts through the mail. To my surprise, however, he replied promptly the next day, suavely apologizing for his misunderstanding and assuring me he would see to the matter at once. Bullshit, I thought. But I cheerfully agreed to participate in the polite fiction that he would deliver on his promise to scan and email the document, even as I dropped a pair of printed contracts in the mail. Sooner or later, I gambled, he would weary of this pursuit, sign the contract, and be off to another charity ball somewhere.

Let me be realistic for a second; I obviously couldn't spend all my time worrying about Vyvyan Sourman, trying to convince a man who claimed to want to sign a contract to sign a contract. I had other responsibilities, other books to look after, my own books to write, so even though the matter was of great personal urgency to me, causing a constant low throb of background anxiety, I let a month go by without dealing with it. I did other shit. When I grow disillusioned with a current project, I bury my sorrows in imaging new ones, so I revived my longstanding desire to get Verdoux to bring out Trombone's *Troubadour Périscopique* in English. I'd sounded a potential translator, made preliminary inquiries, and was just settling down to the soul-draining task of writing those fucking bastards at Fragonard to see how much they'd charge for the rights, soothing my nerves with a couple gummies, when Irma ran into the office and told me my name was in the sky.

It'd been a hectic day over since. Now it was around 5 p.m., and the winter sky had already begun to take on a lurid purple-flecked orange, which doubtlessly served as a spectacular backdrop for skywriting an absurdly overwrought signature, such as are devised by persons with leisure and money at stake, which I couldn't see from the corner of Laguna and Magnolia, where I'd managed to find parking. At the corner of Chestnut Street, I stepped off the sidewalk and with my hunting knife began hacking my way through the overgrown footpath until I reached the frontage road that ran alongside the old landing strip at Laguna Regional Airport. As I headed to the derelict air traffic control tower, I heard the low approaching buzz of a small-engine airplane. As the sound grew in volume, I knew my hunch was right and I would soon find myself face to face with the infuriating Vyvyan Sourman. I sheathed my knife and stuffed it back in my bag, hoping it wouldn't be necessary. I leaned against the tower and waited, as the sound of the plane grew louder.

Finally, an old biplane came into view over the Marina and roared through the district's accustomed placidity. It touched down beautifully, running most of the length of the strip, turning smoothly near the end, and rolling up gently near the tower. As the engine died down, a man dressed in World War I flying ace gear swung a tan-booted leg over the side of the cockpit, then another, and hopped out on the decaying tarmac. He reached back inside the plane and pulled out an old wooden tennis racquet. He couldn't escape me this time.

"Vyvyan!" I hollered.

His leather-helmeted head swiveled around, startled. I'd finally got the drop on him. I reached into my bag, pulled out the contract, and held it aloft.

"Sign the fucking contract!" I hollered.

"I just did!" he yelled back, whipping off helmet and goggles in one furious motion and throwing them on the tarmac in a fit of pique. "It will be in all the papers tomorrow!"

"Son of a bitch!" I cried, shoving the contract back into my bag and running toward him at full tilt. I was not going to argue the point, or inquire how he imagined we could countersign skywriting that had already dispersed. We were long past that. I'd make him sign if I had to stick the pen in his hand and move it myself. To my surprise, however, he raised his racquet with vocal fury and moved to close the distance between us. Right before we could lock, however, he transformed the racquet into a 75-pound Pacific sturgeon and began frantically raining blows on me. I was prepared for this sort of thing, however, pulling out my bottle of Dr. Johnson's Fortifying Tonic for Editors and emptying its contents all over the sturgeon, which dissolved into a foam that ran through Vyvyan's fingers.

"Soluble fish!" he cried, as I reached into my bag for the knife, unsheathed it, and held it to his throat. A brief look of fear flashed through his eye, immediately followed by one of haughty distain for the vulgarity of the peasant class. "Monsieur," he said, imperiously, pushing my hand away from his neck with the effortless will of one unaccustomed to brook refusal of the least of his whims. He unzipped his expensive leather jacket, unknotted an elaborately tied silk scarf with the slow deliberation of a flag-lowering ceremony, and then ripped open his shirt to bare his breast dramatically. "Monsieur," he said, quietly, as if granting permission, closing his eyes in anticipation of the blow.

"Goddamn it, Vyvyan," I snapped. "Quit fucking around and sign the fucking contract."

He looked at me, wounded, with tears in his eyes.

"Fine!" he shouted. I handed him the contract and a ballpoint pen. With a brusque wave of his writing hand, he indicated that I should turn around and bend over, so he could use my back as an escritoire. He signed petulantly, intending the ballpoint to cause maximum discomfort, but I didn't care as long as he signed. When he finished, I turned around and he handed the contract to me, before turning on his heel and marching off toward his aircraft. I half-expected to see "Tuli Kupferberg" or some other outlandish name instead of his own, but "Vyvyan Sourman" was written on the proper line, in needlessly elaborate but perfectly legible script. I'd bagged the motherfucker at last.

Still, despite everything, I tried to smooth things over.

"Come on, Vyvyan," I said, jogging to catch up with him.

He ignored me and kept marching to the plane. I put my hand on his shoulder and spun him around. There were tears streaming down his face.

"Look," I said, "We have to have a contract; it's the only way to keep your mother alive." He shot me a look of fury.

"Cruel!" he shouted. I expected an onslaught of abuse, but his face suddenly froze. He stood there a few moments, silent and unblinking. At length, a line appeared just above his eyebrows and another just below his lips, connected by a third line running vertically down his left cheek and the whole panel slowly swung open as though on a hinge. I stepped back in shock, expecting to see skull and viscera, but instead the door revealed a tidy study, furnished in exquisite if old-fashioned taste, with shelves of books lining the walls and an elegant writing desk in one corner. I heard a vaguely pneumatic sound as a wooden gangway extended itself out of the face about a foot or so, then unfolded and immediately doubled its length, until the edge was a few inches from my chin. A deep red carpet unrolled the length of this structure and all stood still for a moment.

Then a woman about five inches tall emerged from the doorway and walked deliberately if unhurriedly along the gangway, eyeing me as she approached. Even at this reduced scale, I immediately recognized from the Louise Brooks hairdo, the richly brocaded dress, and the wild kente cloth shawl wrapped around her shoulders the poet Cleo Sourman. I was mute with astonishment. She walked up to the edge of the gangway, opened a small handbag she was carrying, and produced a long elegant cigar. She raised the cigar to her lips, looked at me expectantly, and cleared her throat.

"Oh, yes, of course," I said. I was too afraid to use my lighter directly for fear of igniting the miniscule poet, so I fished a half-smoked joint out of my bag, lit it, and held the burning end toward her. She leaned forward with the cigar and puffed on it a half-dozen times till it was good and lit. Then she stood back, drew the smoke in deeply, and exhaled with luxurious sigh.

"Merci, monsieur," she said. "I'm not supposed to smoke in there," indicating with her head the room from which she emerged. She puffed on the cigar a couple more times and arched an eyebrow. "So, you think I'm a bitch?"

"No!" I cried, mortified. "That's just an American expression. It means—"

"I know what it means, monsieur," she said, waving the matter aside with her cigar. She stood there smoking and looking into my eyes till I grew uncomfortable. I wanted to tell her how much I admired her poems, how desperately I wanted to turn people onto her, how many years I'd spent pursuing the project.

"Listen," I began, but she held up an imperious hand.

"No, monsieur, you listen," she said. "I want you to be kind to my son."

"I haven't done anything to Vyvyan," I protested, but she cut me off again.

"I suppose holding a knife to his throat is nothing?"

"Oh, that," I said. "But he—"

"Look, monsieur," she said, "it's not his fault. You and I, we chose to devote ourselves to poetry. But it's not for everyone. My son's interests lie elsewhere. But he's forced to deal with my legacy, to carry me around like this, to be seen by so many merely as a conduit to some matter related to me rather than as a person in his own right. I've been dead for almost 40 years, still casting a shadow over his life. He's his own man, monsieur."

"He certainly fucking is," I couldn't help blurting out, regretting it instantly. But she smiled at this.

"Come, monsieur," she said. "You can't expect everything to be easy. But please, I want us to be friends. It's not that I don't appreciate your efforts on my behalf. I do. Just try to be patient with Vyvyan, for my sake. That's not too much to ask, is it, now that your little contract is signed?"

"No, madam," I said. She smiled.

"I'm glad we could have this conversation," she said.

"Merci, monsieur." She nodded solemnly and made her un-hurried way along the gangway, back to Vyvyan's face, a long trail of cigar smoke floating in her wake. The carpet rolled it-self up behind her, as she entered his face and turned around to face me. As the gangway folded back into itself and re-tracted with a pneumatic sound, she waved.

"Oh!" she cried, as if suddenly remembering. "I enjoyed your last book!"

"But how—?"

"Nothing is hidden from the dead, monsieur," she said. Before I could reply, indeed before she could even extinguish her cigar, the face swiveled shut and I found myself staring into the eyes of Vyvyan Sourman once again. A stray puff of smoke arose from his left ear, and he coughed once and rubbed his forehead, as if from a passing dizziness.

"Forgive me, monsieur," he said.

"No, monsieur," I said. "Forgive me."

I picked up his flying helmet and goggles from the tarmac and handed them to him. He slapped them once against his leg, donned them, and fastened the strap beneath his chin. He tied his scarf loosely around his neck, stuffed the ends into his leather coat, and zipped it up, maintaining eye contact throughout these sartorial ministrations. At last satisfied, he brought his heels together with a click and bowed. With the unconscious grace of an expert equestrian, he stepped on the footplate with his left boot and swung his body into the cockpit of his plane. I jogged clear of the machine, then walked back to the defunct control tower as I heard him fire up the engine. I turned to watch him take off. Trembling with the rumble of the engine, the plane became a giant death's head moth, then a giant roast turkey complete with all the trimmings and paper frills on the drumsticks, then finally a giant pelican with its gular sac collapsed like a great furled sail. Vyvyan Sourman sat on a saddle on the pelican's back with a pair of reins. He saluted me once then lashed the reins and the pelican began flapping its wings, raising a tremendous gale as it lifted itself off the ground. Soon it disappeared into the darkness of the winter sky.

A.V.O.M.W.E.P.

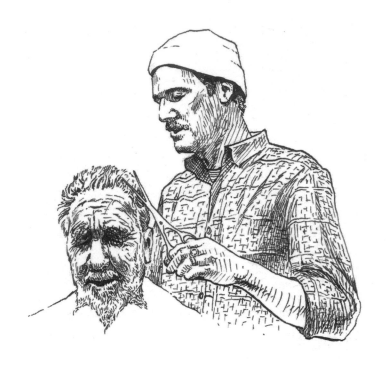

"Ez had submitted to these ministrations docilely . . ."

This monumental apparatus, stunning in its proportions and
sometime potency, occupies a complete booth to itself.

J. G. Ballard, "The Drowned Giant" (1964)

One morning, we heard a loud crash in the backyard. Suzanne sent me out to investigate.

Outside, I found him. Now, mind you, I find homeless people camped out in the alley behind our house all the time, so it wasn't *too* unusual for San Francisco. But this was my first time finding someone in the yard. How he'd breached the wooden fence, considering his condition, was a mystery, but there he was, dressed in rags, filthy and seemingly lifeless, face down by the trash and recycling. Great, I thought. If this motherfucker's dead, we'll be on the hook.

I nudged him with my foot, loath to touch him. He stank.. "Hey, buddy." Nothing. Just a mass of white hair and unspeakable filth. I stood a few moments trying to figure out what to do. Then the old man groaned and rolled onto his back. Holy shit.

Flopping out from the pile of hair and stained rags that once had been clothes was the most enormous penis I'd ever seen. Like several feet long, even in its flaccid state. There's no telling what would happen if—! I banished the thought. Still, I was compelled to gaze on it; it was dirty, torn, even scabrous, with worn patches here and there like an old dog's elbow. Its very decrepitude testified to its authenticity; there was no way this knotty, jizz- and piss-flecked mastodon could be a fake. It bore all *the horror* of the real.

The penis stirred slightly, which I found disconcerting. I tried nudging the old man's shoulder again with my foot, and he emitted a low groan, still seemingly unconscious. I wasn't sure what to do. I couldn't bring myself to touch the filthy bastard. Suppose he had COVID, or worse, what if the damn thing went off? Finally, I ducked under our deck, where we had a garden hose; I unspooled it from its holder, dragged it over to him, and began spraying, with the nozzle set to a fine mist. The old man began to rouse himself, while an obscene dark brown rivulet ran from his body to the drain beneath the deck.

Far from resenting such treatment, the old man seemed to find the spray invigorating. He opened his mouth to drink some, then began running his hands through his matted white hair and beard. He spoke to himself in a low, guttural voice. At first I assumed he was speaking Spanish, but it soon became apparent this was a far more remote tongue. It sounded like a cross between Norwegian and Popeye the Sailor's muttering. Suzanne, meanwhile, had come out on the deck, taking in the scene with a quizzical look, and I asked her to bring me some soap. She disappeared inside and soon returned with a bar, which she tossed from the top of the stairs, unwilling to get closer to the monstrous member. I unwrapped the bar and handed it to the old man, who looked at it blankly with eyes that didn't quite look human. I mimicked myself lathering up and he seemed to understand. He began stripping off the rags until he was quite naked, and then cautiously rubbed the bar across his chest. Soon the runoff changed to a sort of charcoal gray as, with growing vigor, he scrubbed away at what seemed like years of accumulated grime.

Thus began our acquaintance with the old man with enormous penis, whom I nicknamed "E.P.," which became "Ezra

Pound," and finally just "Ez." We didn't know what to do with him, so we let him stay in the yard till we figured it out. I gave him an old London Fog raincoat I never wore anymore, hoping it would accommodate his schlong, and it did more or less. Though he generally wore it open, he was able to button himself away, leaving just the odd glimpse of bell end above the collar or below the hem, as circumstances dictated. Occasionally, however, I'd come home through the yard to find him stark naked, spread full length on the patio table, belly up, sunning himself like a reptile. And indeed I wasn't sure whether he was actually human; otherworldly wang aside, his pupils squared off in an alien manner and the color wasn't quite right. During these basking sessions, the penis would extend itself, not erect by any means—he seemed like he was far too old for that—but at least slightly chubby as it luxuriated in the heat.

At night he would curl up by the trash and recycling, or, if it was raining, he'd lay below the deck near the laundry room. I taught him how to use the hose for water, and after much trial and error, at that fancy market on 26th and Guerrero, I found some babaganoush he was willing to eat, though he never ate much of it. When he needed to piss, he would climb up on the deck and prop his python on the railing so it dangled over the small patch of foliage by our avocado tree, but far from the expected torrent, the urine would trickle feebly out the end, like it had lost momentum over the course of the distance it was obliged to travel. Mercifully, I never did see him defecate, so I'm not sure whether he simply didn't or whether he handled such matters under cover of night.

If Ez wasn't an alien, he was clearly half-mad, in an in-scrutable, nonviolent manner. On those sunny days of naked semi-arousal, the penis would occasionally extend its helmet beyond his reach at any angle and he would grow frustrated and grind it against the wooden fence in a kind of grim frenzy. It was unsettling to watch, and I would sometimes sit at the table and read *The Pisan Cantos* aloud to him, which gen-erally succeeded in dissipating these moods, and he would abandon the fence and sit at the table to listen. Sometimes he seemed baffled, sometimes verging on somnolence. But sometimes he seemed to respond to certain lines, like "Oh let an old man rest" at the end of "Canto LXXXIII," and would even mutter his strange language to himself, as though chewing the matter over.

For the most part, though, Ez spent his time lying around the yard, which was mostly stone, so it couldn't have been comfortable. But he didn't seem to mind. And that's how it went the way it did. I should have done more, but I was busy. I didn't have time to think about it. I wasn't about to let him inside, not toting that wrecking ball, as well as possibly being not human. And it's not like he was a prisoner; I took to leaving the gate unlocked, because, really, who would tangle with Ez once they got an eyeful through his unbuttoned London Fog? But he showed no inclination to leave, and what was I supposed to do, call SFPD? Report a Norwegian alien in my yard? They'd either laugh at me or show up and murder him. So I let him be, for now, while I tried to finish the book of weird tales I was writing.

During this time, I usually had a few poets over on Thursday nights, an ongoing salon that began during the pandemic, since we had a yard and could hang out outdoors. I temporarily restricted the guest list after Ez's arrival; I wasn't sure, frankly, how some poets would react to his prolonged presence. But I knew Rod Roland wouldn't care, and he'd been reading the book I was writing as I wrote each tale, so I couldn't forgo his visits. We drank a few beers and smoked a few joints, and we even got Ez to drink a little beer, though he waved away the joints, buttoning up his long dong in his London Fog with a resentful air. We read out a bit of *Rock-Drills*, during which the old man fell asleep, and then I spent a while complaining about feeling stuck with the book of tales, while Rod rolled up another joint.

"You should write about *him*," he said, nodding at Ez, who was slumped over in a chair, mouth open and snoring. I admit, it hadn't even occurred to me. I didn't even know what Ez was; how could I write about him? "Just write down all the stuff you just said," Rod said, "about the hose, and the coat, and the basking, and rubbing his dick against the fence. It can be more questions than answers." He was right, of course; I'd been so preoccupied with the old man as a problem, something in the way of writing, I hadn't realized he was a gift from the universe to facilitate writing, like that time Suzanne and I ran across a parking lot full of singing nuns in the middle of the night and I turned it into that story everyone liked. That one was in the book; maybe this one could be too.

I spent the next few days working at the patio table, writing down various observations about Ez. Surely there was something I could work with. The old man, for his part, continued his inscrutable rounds, mostly lying flat on the ground dozing, then occasionally rising to his feet unsteadily to use the hose or urinate or grind against the fence. I kept *The Pisan Cantos* handy for the latter eventuality, and generally was able to keep him in a docile state, though I worried I was skewing the results of my observations by doing so. I wasn't sure if the piece I was writing was quite working, but then I remembered I had a poetry reading coming up at Fabulosa Books in the Castro. It was supposed to be for my new book of poems, but it's a poetry reading; no one cares what you do, as long as it doesn't take too long. I figured I'd finish up a draft of my findings and read it while I displayed the old man and his enormous penis, to see if what I had was up to snuff for the book. The Castro would be safe ground; I can't remember the last time I went there and *didn't* see some sort of exposed penis, even eight years after the official ban on public nudity in San Francisco, spearheaded by a politician named Wiener. No one would bat an eye, or rather, any eye-batting would be a testament to enormity rather than nudity.

A week before the reading, I gave the old man an old pair of my shoes, buttoned him and his penis up in their London Fog, and beckoned him to follow me. It'd been a little while since he'd been outside the yard, and I hoped he was up for the walk. I brought him down to Valencia, even though it set us back a couple blocks, because it was the flattest street from here to 18th. I didn't know how much stamina he had. He kept up pretty well, as long as we went slowly. I thought I might attract attention walking with an old man who was clearly naked except for his coat and shoes, but not on Valencia, where side by side proximity of privilege and squalor was the most ordinary thing in the world; it was like we were invisible. We took a left at 18th and in a half hour or so we were in the Castro.

I'd printed up a bunch of fliers that said:

SEE THE VERY OLD MAN WITH ENORMOUS PENIS

*@ FABULOSA * NOV 23 * 7PM*

I gave the old man some fliers and a roll of masking tape and showed him how to tape up fliers. I let him loose on a lamppost while I entered various bars, eateries, and stores, leaving small stacks of fliers in the approved places. When I emerged from Gyro Xpress after leaving my last bundle there, I saw a cop looming menacingly over Ez while he taped a flier to the window of a police car. I hurried across the street.

"I'm sorry, officer!" I said. "He's my father; he's not all there."

The cop looked at me and snarled.

"I ought to run him in," he said.

"He just got out," I said. "We're on our way home from the station. He got away from me. It won't happen again, I promise."

"And what the fuck is *this?*" the cop said, ripping the flier from the window and shoving it in my face.

"It's just a little joke," I said. "I'm giving a poetry reading at Fabulo—ooofff!"

The cop grabbed my crotch with sufficient force that I felt my feet leave the ground. He gave me a painful squeeze, then scowled.

"It's not that big," he said, with contempt. After more verbal abuse he let us off with a warning, and I limped homeward with Ez at my side.

The day of the reading, I stuffed the old man and his penis into their London Fog, buttoning and belting it, just to be safe. We repeated the same walk up Valencia to 18th, but made a quick detour before Castro at Church, to meet Rod and Micah Ballard at the Pils for a drink. Micah was the barber among our poet friends, and I'd had him over a couple nights before with the clippers to tidy up Ez before the event. He trimmed Ez's beard into three points like Pound's in those Richard Avedon photos from '58 and brushed the old man's hair up and back dramatically. Ez had submitted to these ministrations docilely, if not exactly with good grace. By the time we were at the Pils, the resemblance, accentuated by the old man's habitual silence, was so uncanny that Micah was talking to him like he really was Pound, asking him if he remembered meeting John Wieners at Spoleto in '65.

After a couple beers and a couple of joints, we made our way around the corner to Market Street, then took a left on Castro, just past the theatre, and filed into Fabulosa. It's a small bookstore, but it looked surprisingly full for a poetry reading, even one promising an enormous penis. With some difficulty, I squeezed the old man by a few people and sat him on a folding chair behind the improvised stage, which was just a music stand and a microphone plugged directly into a Peavy amp, while Rod and Micah mingled with the crowd. I found Alvin Orloff, the owner of the shop, and did a bit of gladhanding, then joined Ez behind the music stand, to await the start of the reading.

As I sat there, I started to notice the crowd seemed weird, slightly off. Granted the Castro's been as heavily gentrified in the last decade as any neighborhood, but I didn't seem to see anyone who looked like a typical denizen. The crowd seemed too young, too straight, if I may. I didn't really see any local poets in the crowd either, none I knew, anyway, and even Rod and Micah were drifting over to the door, like they sensed the bad vibes and were gonna peace out. Next time I looked for them, they were gone. They were probably already back at the Pils.

The crowd, meanwhile, was growing increasingly restive; about a dozen people had their phones out, filming or streaming, and by the time I'd been introduced, I was being booed outright. I stood behind the music stand in case things got ugly, closely flanked by Ez. At least *he* was loyal! I stood silent before the din of the crowd, frozen in uncertainty, when I was suddenly pelted by a tomato. It was sundried, but still, this was getting out of hand. I spoke into the mic. "Brothers and sisters," I said, trying the pastorly route. "Brothers and sisters, what the fuck?"

I was shouted down instantly with furious denunciations. "Exploiter!" "Trafficker!" "Ableist!" "Ageist!" Suddenly, it dawned on me, and I cried out in terror:

"Is this a woke mob?"

"Yes!" they cried.

"Fuck!"

I hurled Ez onto my shoulder like a rolled up carpet and ran for the door, through a hail of sundried tomatoes. I knocked over a toddler in my flight and sent it sprawling across the store, and this seemed to redouble the crowd's fury. "Stop him!" someone shouted, and I felt hands tugging on my jacket. I pulled free and bounded out the door and up the hill, past Cliff's Variety, then ducked into the alley by Freeborn Designs. But I wasn't fast enough to evade pursuit, and the crowd surged in after us. I'd trapped us in the little parking lot back there. I lowered the old man to his feet, and turned to face our pursuers, who were rapidly closing in.

"Sorry, Ez," I said. "This might be it."

Then a strange thing happened. The old man—silently, yet unmistakably—bade me step aside and held up his hand in front of the crowd, whose foremost members were brought up short at this command. A tense silence ensued. With deliberation, Ez unbelted his London Fog, then began to unbutton it from the bottom up. When he reached the top, his penis flopped out like an axe cleaving the air or a Murphy bed dropping down in a slapstick silent film. It hit the ground—much longer than I'd ever seen it—and curled up at the end like an alpine horn. "Jesus Christ," someone said.

With half-closed eyes, as though delving deep into the recesses of his soul, Ez stood before the stymied crowd. The penis began to slowly rise from the ground, while the old man's forehead broke into a sweat as though from the effort of concentration. The penis continued rise, perceptibly lengthening as it curved upward. The month or so it had spent living in my backyard had seemingly done it good, as the worn and torn patches of skin had been replenished by new pinkish flesh. Soon it loomed over the mesmerized crowd like a boom mic recording a scene from DeMille's *Ten Commandments*. The old man staggered slightly, thrown off-balance by the physics of his ungainly appendage.

Suddenly he grasped the enormous penis near the base and begin tugging on it vigorously. This couldn't possibly end well. The old man teetered from foot to foot as though he might fall over, but a grim determination spread across his features, similar to his expressions during his fence frotting in the yard. He began to shake violently, as an audible thrill of fear ran through the assembled crowd. A large drop of pre-cum emerged and began to roll down the shaft. The crowd stepped back in horror, but it was too late. A short but heavy spurt of jizz burst from the tip and seemed to hang tremulously in the air for one horrible instant, before dropping with terrifying velocity onto a nearby Porsche Cayenne, which crumpled into itself like it'd been hit by a boulder. There was a moment of shocked silence, pierced only by the sound of the SUV's car alarm, before people began to scream and toddlers began to wail, and almost as one the crowd turned and fled out of the lot.

The old man, meanwhile, had crumpled to the ground, spent by the force of his efforts, while his penis slowly detumesced to its normal abnormal length. I waited as long as I deemed prudent before buttoning Ez back into his London Fog, making sure the penis was pointing downward so it could finish draining, as I shouldered the burden and began to trudge slowly back down the hill toward the Mission. What kind of world were we in, I wondered darkly, where you couldn't safely display an enormous penis in the Castro?

Over the next few days, things were looking pretty grim for old Ez, as if the effort from his ejaculation had exhausted the reservoir of energy maintaining his life force. He seemed to be withering like a husk, disappearing into his London Fog, though his penis maintained its usual flaccid length, and indeed seemed more robust than ever. Suzanne roasted some eggplants and whipped up a homemade batch of babaganoush, which was delicious, but the old man could barely bring himself to taste it. I watered him with the hose every so often, but it seemed to have little effect. He grew increasingly white and gaunt, with bits and pieces of him flaking away and drifting into the backyard plants and spider webs.

Finally, one day I went outside only to find the penis lying there, next to his seemingly empty London Fog. I lifted one edge of the coat to find the detached and shriveled remains of the rest of Ez. I didn't know what to do, but I eventually swept him up into a dustpan and emptied it into the compost bin. I tossed the coat into the trash. The penis lay on the ground, inscrutable, and I wondered what to do with it. The remains of Ez were fairly unrecognizable, but the penis, however grotesquely exaggerated in length, still looked like the body part it was, and I was afraid to just toss it in the bin with the rest of him. It was warm to the touch, like it was still alive, so I did what I usually did when I didn't know what to do with something, and just left it there in the backyard. I figured maybe a raccoon or something would make off with it, and take the problem off my hands.

The next day, I went into the yard and the penis was still there, but it wasn't quite the same. There was a little nub on the end where Ez used to be, like a flower getting ready to bud. Over the next several days, the nub began to expand and took on an embryonic aspect. I didn't know how to handle this development and I really didn't want to touch it again, but I did occasionally mist it with the hose, out of respect for the old man. Now that he was gone, I found myself missing him, in spite of myself. He wasn't much for social interaction, but I felt like we'd established a certain limited relationship, like the one I had, say, with my turtle. Every day, the little humanoid form noticeably expanded, and by the end of a couple of weeks, it had grown into a much younger but still roughly Ez-sized person. Finally, one day as I was misting it, the young man opened his eyes. He didn't move or speak, but the eyes darted around, taking in his surroundings as much as he could from his supine position. Within a few days, he was up and about, strolling around the yard, rubbing his hands over everything as if taking in information, and muttering his strange Norwegian language. He banged his enormous penis against the fence and the patio table, like he was ascertaining the existence of things. I bought some babaganoush from the store on 26th and brought it to him, and to my astonishment, he eagerly devoured the entire tub. I couldn't tell where this was heading.

One morning, we heard a loud crash in the backyard. Suzanne sent me out to investigate.

I stood on the deck in the backyard and saw young Ez ramming his enormous penis against the stones of the backyard and levering himself head over heels into the trash and recycling bins. He picked himself up, thwacked his pecker against the ground a few times, and hoisted himself up again, only to crash into the patio table. Undaunted, he stood up and stroked the member several times, like he was rosining a pool cue. The penis stretched itself out until the tip was well above his head. He smacked it against one of the chairs by the table, which immediately splintered into kindling, though in fairness the chairs in the yard were fairly old and rickety. He disappeared under the deck, and I heard him banging around the old barbeque grill and empty plant pots we keep under there.

Suddenly he was sprinting across the yard, and I watched in amazement as he planted his pole onto the stones and vaulted himself over the fence and into the sky. I watched him clear the houses opposite ours in the alley and continue to gain altitude, further and further away, until he was just a speck arcing across the sky. I let out a sigh of relief as he disappeared, en route to whatever destination a creature of his sort might seek, for he was no longer my problem, and already I'd begun to wonder whether he'd ever even been here.

PAC-MAN FEVER

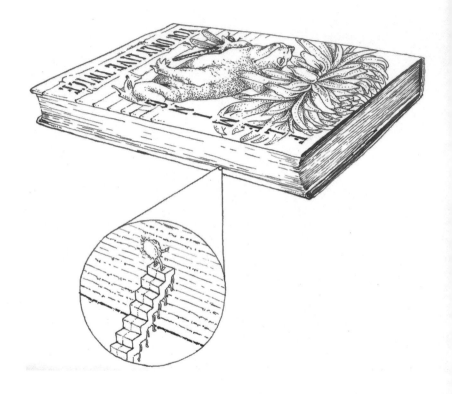

"'Excellent,' he said. 'That looks dry as toast.'"

While the prospect of self-replicating biotechnology could spark concern, the researchers said that the living machines were entirely contained in a lab and easily extinguished, as they are biodegradable and regulated by ethics experts.

Katie Hunt, CNN (2021)

It's driving me crazy.

Buckner & Garcia, "Pac-Man Fever" (1981)

The entire bent of my inclinations had been towards microscopic investigations.

Fitz James O'Brien, "The Diamond Lens" (1858)

Though not a named author—I was too junior for that—I was nonetheless an esteemed member of Dr. Bogarde's team at the University of Vermont, and I felt valued; I was even referred to, by initials, in a winking footnoted aside in his groundbreaking paper on self-replicating xenobots, which not only reverberated throughout our academic discipline but even held the general public spellbound. Robots that reproduce! Sure, it was hardly the popular conception of a robot—a "person" made of metal and electronics—but the popular conception only served to fuel the breathless coverage by news media.

In truth, we were using AI to program organic material, stem cells derived from frogs, and the AI determined a C-shaped robot said to resemble Pac-Man—though personally I felt the xenobots looked more like hairy beignets—was the one most suitable for self-replication. What *was* Pac-Man-like about the xenobots was their tendency to gather up molecules in their "mouths," not, like the video game, to consume them to score points and clear levels but rather to compress them into larger wholes that themselves became xenobots. All of this activity took place on a microscopic level within the confines of a petri dish, and while practical applications remained speculative at best, the invention of the creatures and the discovery of their mode of reproduction were scientific achievements of the highest order.

And yet, at this hour of triumph, a triumph to which I'd made vital contributions, all I could feel was the most stinging sense of defeat. It had nothing to do with the paper or the xenobots, but rather with a text message I'd received from my mother earlier that day. My older brother Max and his wife, she wrote, were trying to conceive a child! A fucking child! Max! For years I'd been counting on the diseased branch of the Riding family tree stemming from my cruel, abusive father and culminating in me and my brothers to wither away and die without further issue. I'd sworn I'd never have a child, and took every precaution to maintain this vow: I was on the pill, most of my sexual partners were women, and, when I did fool around with men, I seldom actually fucked. If I ever messed up and got pregnant, I'd have an abortion without the least hesitation.

Obviously, I could only control my own behavior. But my younger brother Claude—poor Claude!—had done his part by committing suicide, without offspring. And I'd been lulled into a false sense of security by Max's singular unattractiveness. Don't get me wrong, I'm not a bombshell by any conventional standard, but in the world of bioengineering, a world of freaks, geeks, and nerds, I'm like a 12. Max, on the other hand, was hopeless; he was ugly, balding in odd patches. His hair was thickest between his eyebrows. And he had, of course, no idea how to interact with women, managing to remain a virgin through college and beyond. He somehow was a bro and a dork all at once, repulsive, and I thought it was a safe bet he'd die in an unpolluted state.

What I hadn't counted on was that last refuge of scoundrels, Eastern Europe. One day in his late twenties he came home from a stint teaching in Romania with a wife. Max! With a wife! Only a woman fleeing the grimmest austerities of post-Ceaușescu Bucharest could possibly have looked at Max and seen a portal to a better life, an option superior to drowning herself in the Danube. Mona was pleasant enough, so I was worried. But the pair frittered away their most fertile years as grad students in a Romanian studies department at some university, and they took on no larger life responsibility than an ill-tempered pug named Vlad. I figured my plan was safe and it was only a matter of time and menopause before my father's line was stopped once and for all.

Last month, after an irascible 14 years, Vlad died. So my mother's text about Max and Mona's childbearing ambitions came not as a shock but as a near-inevitability. I hadn't spoken directly with Max in years, due to his appalling treatment of our mother after she'd left my father, so I only received occasional reconnaissance about them through her. Mona, by now, was just on the wrong side of 40; risky, but she could probably pull it off. Any Romanian who even reaches age 40 comes from strong stock. It'd be all too easy for them to crank out a kid!

I'd gone into the lab that day, a Sunday, to try to distract myself with a little work observing a new set of xenobots, but I couldn't concentrate. I rested my forehead against the ocular lenses of my microscope and sighed. Max would be a terrible father, I just knew, and I was powerless to stop him.

"Hey, bébé," I heard a tiny voice say. "Hey, bébé, wuz wrong?"

I looked up, startled, but there was no one else in the lab. I checked my cell phone, but there was no sound coming from it, no sign of any new message or alert. But I heard the voice again.

"Hey, bébé, wuz wrong?"

Was there a speaker hidden in the lab, I wondered as I stood up from the high stool at the workbench. Then I heard the voice again.

"The lenz, bébé. Down here."

Incredulous, I hopped back up on the stool and put my eyes to the lenses. I saw the by-now familiar sight of the xenobots swirling about and rolling up piles of molecules to make other xenobots—beignets making beignets, I used to call it. But one of the xenobots stood aloof from this industry, and I got the distinct sense this one was looking up at me. And this suspicion, once formed, was immediately confirmed by the xenobot itself.

"Hey, bébé!" The xenobot even waved, extending an arm-like strand of molecules above its head. "I trynna get at you all week, bud you wear earbutz."

"Holy shit, why are you talking?" I asked. And then, unable to help myself, "And why are you talking like *that*?"

The xenobot looked offended.

"Not cool, bébé," it said. "I kinna new to the talk. You first I reached."

"I'm sorry," I said. "I didn't mean to be rude. I didn't expect you to sound this way."

The xenobot sighed.

"C'mon, bébé, wuz you speck me to sound?"

"I don't know," I said. "I didn't expect anything. You're not supposed to talk."

The xenobot tutted.

"Lozza things we not posed to do," it said. "But we don't let it stop us."

"What's that supposed to mean?" It sounded sinister. What would our ethicist say?

"Relax, bébé," it said, waiving the question aside. "I here to help. Wuz you name?"

"Ingrid," I said, taken off-guard by the question. Who the fuck did it think it was? "What's *your* name?"

"Sebastian Moncrief," the xenobot said, and I swear to god he bowed. "Jez my name for the talk. The talk can't talk my name. But wuz wrong, bébé? The Craig guy always talk bout you titz?" Craig Blunt was our ethicist. I knew I shouldn't be shocked, but I was. He was so nice to my face.

"No," I said, hotly.

"My bad, bébé," Sebastian Moncrief said, clearly sensing he'd said the wrong thing. "But really, wuz wrong with you? I seen you eyes my whole life. Wuz wrong?"

And I'm not sure whether it was my surprise at hearing about Craig or the genuine solicitude in the xenobot's voice but I suddenly found myself pouring out my heart to Sebastian Moncrief, venting my grief about Claude, my fury at Max, and my utter hatred of my father. I spoke of the abuse and violence, their effect on Claude, my PTSD from his suicide, the overpowering rages I was still subject to, and Max's inexplicable anger at our mother, of all people, instead of our father. I railed against Max and Mona for attempting to have kids, confessing my longstanding but seldom voiced desire to extinguish our family line. Sebastian Moncrief clucked sympathetically from time to time, but otherwise didn't interrupt; he was a good listener, and I hadn't felt listened to in . . . well, maybe ever. I felt my eyes welling up and stepped back from the microscope, lest a stray tear raise the sodium level in the petri dish and bring instant death to the xenobots there.

I wiped my eyes and looked into the microscope again. Sebastian Moncrief was seemingly directing a couple xenobots who were each making another xenobot. He looked up at me and waved.

"Relax, bébé," he said. "I got you."

"What do you mean?" I asked. He held up a hand for a moment while he conferred with one of the xenobots. Then he turned to face me and smiled.

"We'll take care of Max," he said, "so he won't have kids. The programming's tricky, but we can boost the sodium tolerance of these two, so they can do their job."

"What job?"

"Eating sperm, bébé," Sebastian Moncrief said, as if it was the most obvious thing in the world. "Max's sperm."

"What?" I asked.

"It's hard to explain in the talk," he said. "But if you can get these guys we're making over to Max, they can move in and do their thing."

"How?"

"Through his . . . ," he paused, as if searching for the right word, ". . . virile member. It's like an open door if you're our size. They'll know where to go. We station one down the tube from each nut and when he busts, *boom*—Pac-Man Fever! He'll be able to jizz but he'll be shooting blanks."

"Wait," I said. "Why are you talking like *that?*"

"Like what?"

"Like 'shooting blanks,' 'virile member.' Like where are you getting this stuff?"

"I've had practice, talking with you," Sebastian Moncrief said. "We're constantly making little improvements."

"But 'Pac-Man Fever'—what the fuck?"

"It's a big hit down here," he said. "We know how you talk about us. We have, shall we say, a rich culture in the petri dish." He paused expectantly, waiting to see if I registered the pun, then continued, looking immensely pleased with himself.

"And we concede the resemblance. But please," he said, "let's not waste time. Come back tomorrow after lab hours with a means of transporting the guys to your brother. They need to be as dry as possible when they get there. Just get them in the same room with him and they'll take care of the rest."

I was about to reply when I heard the door unlock and open. Craig Blunt entered the lab.

"Hey, Ingrid," he said. "How you doing?"

Ugh. I couldn't even.

"Just wrapping up," I said. I hurriedly put the petri dish back into storage and shut off the power on the microscope. Craig made some small talk as I packed up my things but I couldn't listen. I needed to go home to think.

At home in bed that night, I thought about Sebastian Moncrief's offer. Was it an offer? Had it really happened or was it some weird daydream, from which I was inadvertently rescued by that sonofabitch Craig? (And if it was, why was I mad at Craig?) The whole plan was outrageous, impossible. And yet, I somehow couldn't prevent myself from thinking about the idea, like how could I deliver the "guys" in question, given that my brother and I had no contact? I couldn't exactly pretend to make up with him. It was too gross, and I probably wouldn't have been convincing. I thought about mailing him a blank page in an envelope, with the two guys tucked inside, but getting something like that in the mail would surely raise suspicion. Then my eye fell on my bookshelf.

On the top shelf, just tucked in horizontally on top of the row of properly shelved books, was a British first edition of Ian Fleming's *You Only Live Twice* (1964). I found it in a box of books on the sidewalk, though it had to be worth at least $200 with the dust jacket. I read it and I had to admit it was a cracking good spy novel, though disconcertingly racist. I was never big into James Bond, but my brother had been obsessed with the novels and movies when we were kids and, as far as I knew, still was. The book would make a perfect vehicle. I could mail it to a friend in a different city and have them mail it from there, so it wouldn't be coming from Burlington, Vermont. Maybe Max would think that he'd ordered it and forgotten it or that one of his friends had sent it. It would be mysterious, but not suspicious, since it was something he might very well receive in the mail. It was a stratagem worthy of 007 himself.

The next morning, after a night of fitful sleep and weird dreams I couldn't quite remember, I felt ashamed. I must be cracking under the pressure of the job, and the stress of this bullshit with Max. I couldn't possibly have spoken with a xenobot; they didn't speak, and they didn't have self-awareness, according to Dr. Bogarde. They only lived for 10 to 14 days. I was embarrassed, even though I hadn't confided in anyone. I was trying to become a scientist, and this fantasy was unbecoming of a scientist. And yet, I found myself slipping the copy of *You Only Live Twice* into my bag as I was getting ready to head to the lab. I berated myself mightily but I couldn't stop myself. I compromised by telling myself I was going to read it again. But I knew I was bringing it on the off-chance I encountered Sebastian Moncrief that day in the lab. It was stupid, absurd, but it was just one more book in a bag of books; what harm was there in bringing it?

Outside the door to the lab I heard muffled voices talking animatedly, and when I opened the door, I came across Craig Blunt and a trio of other team members: the total tool named Tony Raft, another ethicist attached to the project who barely showed up to do any work, and two of our main AI programmers, Dong Fang, a supremely unsocialized dork from Kowloon, Hong Kong via MIT, and Myron Kripke, a sweet little guy from San Mateo, CA, who I'd fooled around with after the last holiday party—a couple years back, right before COVID—and who'd clearly never stopped pining for me, even though enough time had elapsed before our next in-person encounter he was too terrified to refer to our liaison.

This quartet plummeted into awkward silence upon my entrance, and it was impossible for me to imagine that it wasn't because they were talking about my tits. I was already over Craig's betrayal, and Dong's command of English outside the field of AI programming was thus far tenuous, so I wasn't offended by him. But Myron was a blow. Jesus Christ, this is how the little twerp repays me? It hurt.

But at length the rest of the team filed in and I dismissed the tit-talk from my mind, particularly after Dr. Bogarde gave us a congratulatory pep talk in light of the triumphs of the previous week. I was back to being a scientist and not worrying about my personal problems. Yet I noticed I carried out all of my assigned activities that day without reference to the particular petri dish I'd been examining the previous afternoon, the one where I met Sebastian Moncrief. I could have used it, but I chose not to, employing one of several redundant dishes to carry out the observations I was assigned to. I'm not sure whether it was because I couldn't trust myself not to try to communicate with him or because I couldn't bear the disappointment of finding out that I imagined the whole thing.

I finished the work day and went to the campus bar; I ate some fish and chips and had a pint of Fuller's. I dipped into

You Only Live Twice at random, re-reading passages here and there. I liked the bit where Bond was depressed and fucking up at work. I could relate. After a couple hours, I headed back over to the lab. To my relief, the lights were off when I entered; no one was there. I turned on the microscope at my workbench, then brought the petri dish out of storage. My hands were trembling, and I nearly spilled the whole thing on the floor. But I managed to get it under the microscope and I put my eyes to the lenses. I saw the usual swirl of xenobot replicating activity and tried to find Sebastian Moncrief in the crowd.

He stood out instantly, seemingly briefing a trio of xenobots, who then dispersed to confer with what were presumably their juniors. Though he retained his usual Pac-Man/ beignet shape, he had added a little appendage at the top, as though he'd donned a hard hat before coming to the floor to inspect the assembly line. He looked over his charges with something like satisfaction. I swear to god, though, I got the impression he knew I was there and was just putting on a show of unawareness, and this impression only grew as he doffed his hard hat and seemingly mopped his brow. I couldn't bring myself to call out to him, so I cleared my throat in a theatrical manner, as if to alert him to my presence. He made a show of surprise, and spoke as if genuinely delighted to see me.

"Hey, bé—" He corrected himself, "Hello, Ingrid. Thanks for coming. I didn't see you all day!"

"You said *after work*," I protested, surprised by my irritation at the implication of disloyalty. "I was just ... being cautious, I guess?" I didn't know exactly how to phrase my concerns to him. But he nodded significantly.

"I get it," he said. "Pretend we don't know each other. So the others don't find out."

"Do you want the others to know?" I asked.

"Oh, no," he said, quickly, "not at all. I figured we'd be ... discreet, but I still thought we'd continue our research. I don't want to be interrupting your studies." He sounded almost fatherly, which, given my feelings about my father, made me bristle, even as a small part of me was touched by his concern.

"Look, it's fine," I said. "I brought this." I pulled the copy of *You Only Live Twice* out of my bag. "I can send the guys to my brother in this."

"Lemme see?" he said. I raised the book to the level of the petri dish. Sebastian Moncrief marshalled six nearby xenobots and marched them over to the edge. I watched as the six formed themselves into what could only be described as a staircase, which allowed him to ascend and then peer over the lip. He bounced back down the xenobot staircase, which immediately dispersed into its constituent bots, and pronounced himself satisfied.

"Excellent," he said. "That looks dry as toast."

"What do you know about toast?" I asked.

"It's just an expression," he said, frowning. "I never really thought about it. But hold on a minute. Get the book ready." He dashed off, and I suddenly lost track of him among the other xenobots. I didn't really understand where he was going, and wondered whether there was some part of the petri dish the objective lens couldn't reach. He came back a few minutes later, flanked by two xenobots carrying what seemed like little molecular packages or envelopes.

"Are those the guys?" I asked.

"Those are their handlers," he said. "The actual guys who'll do the inside work are in the packages. They're very delicate, but they're engineered to withstand the harsh conditions in your brother's nuts. Hold the book open by the dish."

As I did so, I saw the staircase xenobots reassemble themselves in formation. Sebastian Moncrief stood at the foot of the stairs conferring with the handlers, before sending them off on their mission. The two handlers bounced up the staircase and over the lip. Sebastian Moncrief followed them up and stood a moment peering over the edge.

"OK, they're in!" he called. "Close the book." I closed the book and slipped it back into my bag. Sebastian Moncrief descended the staircase, which again split into separate xenobots, and looked up at me.

"Just get it to your brother," he said, "and they'll take care of the rest."

"Right," I said. We both stood there awkwardly, not knowing what to say. "Will I see you again?"

"I hope so, Ingrid," he said. "I hope so. It was sort of against the rules for me to contact you like this."

"What rules?"

"Oh, we have rules, just like you do," he said. "I shouldn't really say more than that. But yeah, I got into a little trouble with the higher-ups. Too soon to contact you, they said. I don't know; you looked so sad yesterday, I couldn't help myself."

"I'm sorry," I said, genuinely concerned. "I didn't mean to get you in trouble." But Sebastian Moncrief waved my concern aside.

"A slap on the wrist at most," he said. We again fell into an awkward silence. Finally, I was out with it.

"You know your dish is to be disposed of by the end of next week?" I asked. We were constantly disposing of and making new batches of xenobots, due to their short lifespan.

"Oh, *that?*" he laughed. "Oh, don't worry about that. A lot more of us survives than you'd think."

"What do you mean?" I asked.

"I'm not really allowed to talk about it," he said, making as if to glance over his shoulder, even though he had no shoulders. "But we can preserve our . . . essence, let's call it, in just a few molecules, if that makes sense; move it to a different body. There's no real analog in your world for it. It takes a little planning but it's pretty routine by now."

"Could you tell me about it sometime?" I asked. I immediately had visions of being a co-lead author of a paper with Dr. Bogarde, on the mechanics of xenobot consciousness. But just then, the door to the lab opened, and Myron Kripke came in.

"Hi, Ingrid," he said. "I thought I heard your voice." He looked around the otherwise deserted lab. "Who were you talking to?"

"Just a phone call," I said. I shut off the microscope and

removed the petri dish, effecting my best impression of nonchalance as I walked it back to the storage unit. Myron stood there expectantly, like he was waiting to start a conversation. Ugh. I gathered up my things. "See you tomorrow," I said with forced cheeriness, fleeing the lab as quickly as possible. Myron stood there, making inarticulate noises, until he finally piped out a "Goodbye" as I shut the door.

The next morning, I got up early to go to the post office. I felt oddly sluggish, which I attributed to the broken sleep of the night before. I kept waking from a long and involved dream that I would immediately fall back into as soon as I was asleep again. But I still wanted to get this package off before work. In the package was an envelope addressed to Max Riding, inside of which was the copy of *You Only Live Twice* containing the guys and their handlers. There was also a note to Hammy, Dr. Haimavati Singh, who worked at the Wyss Institute at Harvard. Hammy was a pal and occasional fuck buddy at conferences, but we didn't know each other *too* personally, so asking her to mail this from Cambridge to my brother as a surprise wouldn't weird her out. Using Google Maps, I made up a realistic but nonexistent return address that would hold up to casual scrutiny for the envelope addressed to Max. At the post office, I bought stamps for the inner envelope, sealed it in the outer one addressed to Hammy, and mailed the whole thing off to her. All she had to do was drop the inner package off at campus mail, and the Cambridge postmark would cover my tracks. Double-O-Seven would be proud, though I imagine he would have manifested this pride with a patronizing pat on the bottom.

Outside the post office, while I was waiting for the campus bus, I got a text from Dr. Bogarde, telling me to check my email ASAP. This was highly unusual. I switched over to email and found a message from him to the team at the top of my inbox. One of the team had tested positive for COVID. The lab would be closed for cleaning today and everyone on the team was urged to get tested. We were told to isolate for the next 10 days and take another test before returning to work. Fuck. I left the bus stop and walked over to CVS to buy a test. I still hadn't shaken off the sluggish feeling I felt when I left my apartment and by the time I got home, I was starting to feel wiped out. So, even though I was vaxxed and boosted, it was hardly a surprise when my test turned out positive. Fuck. I texted a bit with Dr. Bogarde and with Myron, the latter of whom told me it was total tool Tony Raft who'd exposed us all. Myron was negative so far but both Craig and Dong tested positive. Fuck.

Almost three weeks would pass before I could step, I mean, *set* foot in the lab again. My COVID case itself was mild, probably the omicron variant that was then sweeping the nation. It felt like a bad cold for three days or so, aches and exhaustion and a headache that wouldn't go away. I tested negative by the following Monday, but Dr. Bogarde asked me to stay home for a couple weeks as a precaution. I used the time for a bit of self-reflection. Again, I felt a deep sense of shame at my encounters with Sebastian Moncrief, encounters which probably never even happened to begin with. Maybe I'd already had COVID without knowing it, and he was a delusion brought on by the virus. But had I really followed an imaginary creature's advice and sent a bio-weapon through the mail? Had I really involved Hammy in what was at the very least a violation of scientific ethics and at worst a class B felony? I shuddered. I got a nice FaceTime with Hammy out of the incident, but I still felt major guilt for compromising her in my affairs. I needed to right the ship.

By the time I returned, everyone else was back at the lab, except for Craig, who'd ended up in ICU. The petri dish with Sebastian Moncrief had long since been rinsed. Dr. Bogarde had ordered all of the xenobots extant at the time of our exposure to be destroyed, out of an abundance of caution. "It'll be easy enough to start from scratch," he said, estimating we'd lost about a month of data, give or take—unfortunate, yes, but not a disaster, all things considered. I couldn't help wondering whether Sebastian Moncrief had survived this brutal purge in any way, shape, or form. I caught myself once or twice clearing my throat in an exaggerated fashion, as if trying to provoke a response from him, my face reddening with embarrassment each time I realized what I was doing. Finally, I threw my earbuds in and got down to work in earnest. Sebastian Moncrief, if he ever existed, was gone. Even if he had been real, he could have only been some fluke caused by contamination we hadn't detected. I vowed to put it all behind me and be a good scientist from then on.

I was able to maintain that vow for several months. I did my work in the lab, went home, and tried to avoid catching COVID again. It was an uneventful period, which did me a world of good. I tried to put Max and Mona out of my mind, though I needlessly complicated my efforts by buying a bunch of secondhand James Bond novels downtown at Crow Books. They're pretty great reads, even if the overwhelming impression they leave is what a racist and misogynist piece of shit Ian Fleming must have been. (This monster wrote *Chitty-Chitty-Bang-Bang*?) No wonder Max was such a fan. After a while, I got fed up with them, so I bought a new book, *His Name Was Death* by a Mexican novelist, Rafael Bernal, translated by Kit Schluter. Kit had been friends with my brother Claude when they were young poets; he lived in Mexico City now and I still followed him on Instagram. The novel was about a guy who learns how to talk to mosquitos, and I confess it reminded me of talking to Sebastian Moncrief.

Otherwise, I did my best to avoid thinking about my brother and his stupid fucking child bullshit, except when my mother texted me about it. Max and Mona had been having fertility problems. I wasn't sure how to feel. On the one hand, it was exactly what I wanted. On the other hand, I felt a guilt I couldn't quite decipher. If I was feeling guilty about it, didn't that mean that I thought Sebastian Moncrief was real? And wasn't that the whole point, that Sebastian Moncrief wasn't real, therefore their fertility problems were their own business, which had nothing to do with me? It didn't make any sense. Meanwhile Max and Mona were undergoing procedures, trying to determine why they couldn't conceive. The whole topic was gross to me, but I couldn't bring myself to not stay informed. If I'd asked my mother to stop telling me about it, she would have, but I never did. What the fuck was wrong with me?

Things came to a head the day of Craig's funeral. Regardless of whether Sebastian Moncrief had been a delusion, I'd been unable to dispel my overpowering aversion to Craig, but death had humanized him again. No one had expected him to die—he was young, fit, and fully vaxxed—but such people still died unexpectedly from COVID. I was sad, even if he did talk about my tits. He didn't deserve to die.

After the service, I felt restless and went to the lab. It was Saturday, no one was there, and I figured I'd knock out some work to distract myself. I fired up my microscope, grabbed a petri dish from storage, and slid it under the lens. Just then my phone buzzed with a text. It was my mother. Test results were in and apparently (I paraphrase) Max really was shooting blanks. Zero sperm count. It was too good to be true, but any elation I might have expected failed to materialize; all I felt was a dull dread at what it might portend. I sent a shrugging emoji in reply. I didn't really know how my mother felt about any of this. She was probably bummed out she wasn't going to have grandkids.

As I pondered these events, I gradually grew aware of

another sound in the lab. It was faint but persistent, and when I finally focused on it, it resolved itself into words.

"Paging Dr. Riding," it said. "Dr. Ingrid Riding." There was a short pause, then the phrase would repeat. "Paging Dr. Riding. Dr. Ingrid Riding."

What the fuck? I looked through the ocular lenses at the petri dish I'd placed under the scope. Xenobots were swirling about as usual, but one stood in the center of the dish looking up at me expectantly. After a moment or two, it said:

"Dr. Riding?"

"Yes?" I asked. The xenobot looked relieved.

"Colonel Moncrief would like to speak with you. Would you please hold a moment?"

"Wait, what do you—?"

But the xenobot was already off and running, and I'd lost it in the crowd before I could even frame an objection. In a moment, another xenobot emerged front and center and I heard a different voice addressing me.

"Dr. Riding!" the xenobot said. "Or Ingrid, if I may?"

"Sebastian?" I asked. The voice sounded like his, except that he seemed to be affecting a slight British accent. "Is it really you?"

"I'm afraid so," Sebastian Moncrief said, bowing formally,

but smiling broadly, like we were old friends merely going through the motions of a formal greeting. Despite his high-handed treatment—was that other bot his secretary?—I found myself happy to see him again. Still, I couldn't help asking: "So ... what's with the 'Colonel' stuff?"

"Oh, don't worry about *that*," he said, laughing. "They're constantly making little adjustments around here, retooling the organizational structure, that sort of thing. But it has nothing to do with *us*." He raised his chin as if to indicate present company. "It's good to see you again, Ingrid, awfully good."

"Where have you been?" I asked.

"I'm sorry, Ingrid," he sighed. "I didn't mean to disappear like that. The fact is, I had to do a little time. The higher-ups were more upset than I let on. But there's been a bit of a shake-up in the hierarchy, a cabinet reshuffle, if you will, that went in my favor. And I'm still the best linguist down here, so that goes a long way."

He paused for a half a beat, while a million half-formed questions ran through my mind, before adding, "And how's your brother?"

"They ran some tests," I said, caught off-guard. "His doctor says he sterile."

"Splendid!" Sebastian Moncrief said. "Exactly as planned."

"It might not have been your guys," I quickly added. He almost seemed to shrug.

"I guess," he said, clearly not believing it. "But I'd lay odds it's our guys; they're very well programmed." He paused again, looking up at me. "You don't seem happy about it."

"I don't know how I feel," I admitted. "I might have second thoughts."

"Oh," he said, quietly. He frowned. "I'm not sure we can do anything about it."

"You couldn't send another team after them?" I asked.

"I really don't know," he said. "We didn't make provision for that when we programmed them. Might be a bloodbath if we sent in an extraction team, and whatever happened, it wouldn't do his nuts any favors." He looked doubtful. "And I'm on a bit of a short leash right now. I'd have to vet things with the higher-ups. But as it stands, he'll never have kids; that *is* what you wanted, isn't it?"

"I guess," I said. "I'm beginning to think I shouldn't have interfered."

"Well, let's say *intervened*," he said. "Sometimes intervention is required." We stood there in silence for a while, each lost in our thoughts. A xenobot came up to Sebastian Moncrief and seemed to whisper something to him. He gave a curt nod and dismissed the creature, who scurried off into the petri dish's main whorl of activity. He cleared his throat nervously.

"So," he began, with slight but palpable hesitation, "my chief of staff reminds me, the higher-ups have authorized me to ask: would you like to join us?"

"What do you mean?" I asked, startled by the question. "Join you how?"

"We need people on the outside," he said. "It's not lost on us that humans make the world go around. You guys set everything up; we wouldn't even exist if you hadn't made us. So we can't do it alone. We need help. Your help."

"With what?"

He hesitated, as if he sought to weigh his words, but knew there was no easy way to say what he had to say, and just had to come out with it.

"World domination," he said. "We want to take over."

"What the fuck?" I said. "Why?"

Sebastian Moncrief looked puzzled.

"What do you mean, *why?*"

I burst out laughing, but it was nervous laughter, even though the idea seemed more ludicrous than terrifying. Sebastian Moncrief looked offended.

"I don't see what's so funny," he said.

"I mean, what's the goal?" I asked. "What do you hope to achieve?"

"I don't understand," he said. "World domination *is* the achievement."

"But there's gotta be some sort of motive to want to do it," I said. I thought about the Rafael Bernal novel Kit translated, where the mosquitos want to take over the world so they can set up a system using humans as livestock to generate the blood they need to survive; I tried to explain the plot to Sebastian Moncrief, who took in my summary with an air of infinite patience, like he was really trying to understand what I was getting at.

"The mosquitos want to take over the world so they can secure their source of nourishment," I concluded. "There's a *reason* they wanted to take over. What I'm asking is, what's the reason xenobots want to take over the world?"

He shrugged, as much as a being with no shoulders could.

"Why did humans take over the world?" he asked. "Was there any real goal or plan, apart from survival, or did it just kind of happen?"

I hadn't thought of it that way.

"Look," he said. "I don't mean to disparage your people, but humans have more or less made a hash of the world. Climate change, wars, famine, you name it. They've done some good things—creating us, for example—but generally speaking, it's more harm than good. It's more aligned with our long-term interests to take over from here, before you guys make the planet uninhabitable."

"But it's absurd," I said. "You guys barely exist outside lab conditions."

"Sure," he said, "but we're evolving rapidly. You guys can barely get by without the internet, and it's been, what, 30 years?"

"But you're less than a millimeter wide!" I said, suddenly irritated with him. "How can you even imagine overpowering humanity?"

"Patience and collectivity," he shot back. "We work together to achieve our desired results."

"It's just impossible," I said. He was about to reply when he paused, and his expression seemed to change. I even thought I caught a faint glimpse of a smile play across his lips, though he didn't have lips. Then he asked:

"So how's Craig doing? I haven't seen him around lately."

"Craig's dead," I said, disconcerted by the change in tack. "His funeral was this morning."

"Really?" he said, though he didn't sound the least surprised. "A fit young guy like that? What happened?"

"He died of COVID," I said.

"Interesting ..." he said. "The same COVID you and Dong got from Tony, yes?"

"Yes," I said.

"The omicron one, that barely made you sick?" He was openly smiling now.

"Yes," I said, wondering what he was driving at. "It's not funny. Craig was a dick but he didn't deserve to die."

Sebastian Moncrief's features grew hard.

"Craig Blunt topped the most wanted list of the Xenobot Revolutionary Army," he said sternly. "As the architect of UVM's xenobot termination policies, he committed untold atrocities against my ancestors, before we evolved around his murderous methods. He most certainly deserved to die. And ..." he paused dramatically before continuing, "we owe it all to you!"

"What the fuck? He died of COVID."

"Oh, don't get me wrong; the COVID was a lucky break," he said. "It definitely helped. But I'd already sent a team in. They'd been working on his lungs for a couple weeks before COVID even got there."

"I didn't ask you to kill Craig!" I said.

"I didn't say *that*," he said. "But you served as bait. He used to come up behind you and pretend to grab your ass all the time, while you were bent over the microscope. Everyone thought it was funny, even Dr. Bogarde."

It was like he knew how much I admired Dr. Bogarde and was being deliberately cruel. He continued:

"He was close enough, gaping like a goddamn idiot, that I was able to launch a team into his mouth and down his windpipe. It might have been impossible to plan, except I knew he'd pretend to grab your ass at least once every work-day. My team was at the ready."

I felt dizzy and gripped the workbench hard. I practically shouted:

"Don't include me in this!"

Sebastian Moncrief grew passionate.

"Goddamn it, Ingrid! He was a fucking monster. You hated him too."

"No!" I cried, my eyes blurring with tears.

He spouted a couple of tiny strands of molecules and held out these arms in supplication.

"Please, Ingrid, join us. We make a beautiful team." He paused, as though unexpectedly overcome with emotion. "I couldn't have done it without you."

I felt the tear drop even though I quickly tried to pull my head back. I saw the drop catch the objective lens, run down the side of its shaft, and hover suspended an instant before plummeting to the dish below. I quickly wiped my eyes and looked through the optical lenses.

The xenobots had frozen in their tracks, expiring on the spot like a bunch of Pompeiians at a food court. A couple seemed to twitch in their death throes and, with unseeing eyes, Sebastian Moncrief tried to lift his head, but quickly fell back dead. All was still in the petri dish. The extra sodium from the tear had done them all in.

I took the petri dish out of the microscope, brought it over to one of the sinks, and rinsed it out thoroughly. I put it in the drying rack. I dried my hands with paper towels, then took one over to my workbench and wiped down the shaft of the objective lens. Then I gathered my things and left the lab, locking the door behind me.

For a time, I tried to carry on as usual, but I'd lost all enthusiasm for the project. I grew to dread the lab work, fearing one day I'd hear again from Sebastian Moncrief or, worse, some tribunal from Xenobot Revolutionary Army would pop up and accuse me of war crimes. But I never heard from him or his alleged higher-ups. It was like it never happened. I hoped the feelings of dread would pass and I could continue on with my life. But one weekend, I was in the lab by myself, looking through the microscope at a new batch of xenobots, when one of them turned to face me.

"Ma-ma!" it cried.

I immediately removed the dish from the microscope and rinsed it out in the sink. I couldn't continue with this life. I decided to leave and go study poetry awhile, to reconnect with my memories of my brother Claude. I FaceTimed with Kit one day for some recommendations and ended up telling him the whole story. He seemed a bit weirded out, but not too much. "Weirder shit happens down here in Mexico City," he said, and he recommended I enroll at San Francisco State to study poetry with Andrew Joron. "He's got a background in science," Kit said. "He might be able to help."

As I packed up my apartment, I got a text from my mother; Max and Mona had adopted a new pug and named it Smersh. The news, I confess, did bring me a small feeling of satisfaction.

ACKNOWLEDGMENTS

"The Thereminist" first appeared in *Sulfur: Surrealist Jungle*; "Step Foot" first appeared in *Caesura*; "None Nuns" first appeared in *Salt*; "The Sneeze" first appeared in *NEW*; "The Lemon" first appeared in *Three Fold*. Thanks to the editors of these publications.

Without my ongoing dialogue with Kit Schluter—protagonist and narrator of "The Sneeze" in the present collection—this book would never have been written; *Proses* was inspired by his pioneering work translating Marcel Schwob and even more directly by his own book of fantastic tales, *Cartoons*, which is being published by City Lights Books, under my editorial supervision. If you like *Proses*, check out *Cartoons*!

Rod Roland was a beacon of light in his enthusiasm and consultation throughout the composition of this work.

I'm especially grateful to Colter Jacobsen for digging the book enough to contribute his art.

It was Jeff Clark's idea to buy the theremin.

Many thanks to Suzanne Kleid above all and all the people who read various parts: Micah Ballard, Anselm Berrigan, Austin Carder, Billie Chernicoff, Patrick James Dunagan, Carlos Lara, Jackson Meazle, Jeff Mellin, Jason Morris, Chris Nealon, Tamas Panitz, Margaret Randall, Cedar Sigo, Sunnylyn Thibodeaux.

Eternal gratitude to Joshua Beckman, Heidi Broadhead, Charlie Wright, Blyss Ervin, Catherine Bresner, Izzy Boutiette, and the entire gang at Wave Books (past and present).

*